As new parents, Matthew and Beth long for a peaceful life with their baby daughter. They get caught up in the aftermath of the disastrous relationship between Gemma Hooper, a promising student, and Janos Farkas, a small-time drug dealer. Intent on using her to expand his evil empire, he transforms her into a glamorous woman.

Determined to turn Matthew's centres for the poor and disadvantaged into outlets for his illegal drugs trade, he is prepared to destroy anyone who stands in his way.

Can Matthew protect Beth as Janos' actions reawaken the horrors of her past? Can their marriage survive as Matthew continually puts his compulsion to do good before the needs of his own family?

Their lives are changed forever as the fallout from Janos' crimes lands at their door.

For Richer or Poorer
Copyright © 2022 S D Johnson
ISBN: 978-1-4874-3589-9
Cover art by Martine Jardin

Published by eXtasy Books Inc

Look for us online at:
www.eXtasybooks.com

FOR RICHER OR POORER

BY

S D JOHNSON

DEDICATION

For my family and Heidi.

PROLOGUE

The nurse wrapped the baby in a soft white towel and placed her into her mother's arms. Beth Thomas thanked her and gazed at the infant, knowing she had never looked at anything so perfect in her life. The bond between mother and daughter was forged in that moment and she felt blessed beyond measure. This was the miracle baby she had longed for.

She had been told it was likely her attacker had robbed her of any chance of motherhood, and yet there she was, her own child in her arms, fathered by the man she loved. He was there, by their side, and he was just as overcome at his first sight of their daughter.

"Hello, Gwynnie," he said, touching her little hand. It clenched instinctively at his touch, the perfect little fingers folding to create a tiny fist. He'd said she looked like a Gwynnie to him, with her incredible mop of dark hair and her beautiful screwed up face.

Beth smiled. He hadn't taken long to shorten their baby's name, but she loved the sound of it. They had chosen the name Gwyneth because it meant miracle, and it paid homage to Matthew's Welsh roots.

"One miracle is enough for me," he'd said.

Beth had beaten the odds by conceiving their baby after the injuries inflicted on her. Her baby had been delivered by C-section, as they had always known she would, but Beth, and now Matthew, had been advised there should be no more babies.

Beth pulled the baby to her gently. She would have filled a

house with children if she had been given the chance, but Matthew was right. Gwynnie was a miracle, and more than she had dared hope for in those bleak old days.

"Has the doctor spoken to you?" she asked.

He nodded. "He said you should be home the day after to-morrow," Matthew said. "I wish I could take you both home right now."

'So do I," Beth said. She thought of the nursery, freshly decorated and equipped. That was for later. Baby Gwynnie was going to have to wait a while before moving into her room, because her mother could not bear the thought of being separated from her.

The old Moses basket, with its fresh mattress and new snow-white drapes, lovingly crafted by Beth, was already at the side of their bed. She reflected that their little one would be the only one in their family to own their own bed. They rented their small cottage fully furnished. One day, she thought, one day, we'll have our own home and our own furniture.

Touching the baby's head with a kiss as gentle as a whisper, she held her towards Matthew as best she could, and he took her into his arms. It was a sight she had never believed she would witness. To say she loved him was an understatement. It didn't come close to describing her feelings for the man who had saved her from her oblivion after the attack. To see him holding their child in his arms was the greatest gift she could have wished for.

He was looking at the sleepy baby the way he looked at her, and she knew he already adored her. This was a moment she had never thought possible, and she wished it could last forever.

CHAPTER ONE

The days Matthew and Beth spent together whilst he was on paternity leave were idyllic. It didn't matter to them that Gwynnie disturbed them six or so times in the night. Each waking proved she was still safe, still healthy, and all theirs.

They stayed home for those precious days, apart from a daily walk to the park. Beth was content to let Matthew go alone for the first couple of days, and then she joined him, walking tentatively, as each step pulled on her stitches.

Matthew was well-known in their village. He was one of the clergy at the parish church, though his paid occupation involved setting up day centres for the needy in towns across the county. It meant that the people who attended the church were eager to greet him and his new baby, and it slowed their progress as they were compelled to stop frequently. These people acknowledged Beth, though they were only vaguely aware of her existence. She chose not to attend church, though she knew she would eventually need to re-examine her feelings, because Matthew would want their baby baptised.

Their precious time together reached its end and he had to return to work, leaving Beth alone with Gwynnie. This presented no fears to her. She had been employed as a nanny before their marriage, and she relished the prospect of looking after her own child.

She hadn't reckoned on the daily stream of visitors. They were the women who had stopped to talk when they had been out walking. She didn't even know their names. They took it upon themselves to visit each afternoon, knowing that Beth would be on her own after Matthew's return to work.

It was Friday afternoon and the fifth time these women had laid siege. Beth looked round the tiny, crowded sitting room and let her mind drift. She tried to block out the chattering of the matronly women who had come to bring their latest offerings of casseroles and cakes.

They weren't bringing their home-cooked offerings for the baby, two weeks old, who was fast asleep in her wicker basket, or for her mother. Everything was for Matthew. They said they had to look after him and make sure he was fed. They seemed to think he was being neglected as she adapted to motherhood. No chance of that, she thought. He was her soulmate, the love of her life. She would die for him.

The aging women in his parishes had always felt the need to mother him. He had an other-worldly, shambolic appearance. He looked as if he needed some new clothes but didn't care enough to buy them, and as if eating regular meals never entered his head. These women thought it their duty to look after him.

They always made the obligatory enquiries about her and Gwynnie's wellbeing, made fleeting admiring comments about the baby, and without waiting for the replies, settled down to their tea, which Beth made. They also set about the cakes they'd brought along and gossiped away as if she was invisible. She knew they would go at around four, leaving their cups and plates on the floor by the side of their seats. She anticipated with resentment the pull on her stitches as she stooped to pick them up.

The bell rang again. Their dog, Sasha, barked furiously, and Beth sighed as she stood to answer the door. She wouldn't be able to find another chair to seat anyone else and she was scared the dog's commotion would wake the baby. She went to the door, every step hurting a little more, yearning for a miracle to give her some peace. She wanted to curl up and spend some time with Gwynnie.

Gemma, a sixth form student at the local college, was at the door. She was delivering her mother's fresh batch of scones and sausage rolls.

"It looks like you're entertaining the coven," she said, having recognised the cars that were parked outside.

Beth allowed herself to raise her eyebrows and roll her eyes.

"Leave it to me," Gemma said.

The girl breezed into the sitting room and greeted the women warmly. They knew of her through the village gossip mill. She instinctively reached down to fuss the dog, who was leaping up and demanding her attention.

"Hello ladies," she said. "Have you all finished your tea? I promised Matthew I would pop in and babysit whilst Beth gets her rest this afternoon. Apparently, she was told to get some rest after lunch." She shook her head at Beth in mock disapproval. "She's been getting herself over tired."

She busied herself collecting cups, taking them through to the kitchen.

Beth noticed with satisfaction that they had taken the hint and were on their feet, picking up their handbags and saying their farewells.

"I'll show you to the door," she said. "It will save Beth getting up."

They left, commenting on what a kind and thoughtful girl she was, oblivious to the deception she had just unfolded in front of them.

"Old biddies," she said, laughing as she went back to the sitting room.

"That was naughty," Beth said with a smile. "I really thought they were settled in for the afternoon. Thank you for saving me."

"They were certainly hunkering down for a long stay," Gemma said. "They mean well, but once they start talking, they get a bit carried away. You do look worn out."

"It gets a bit much," Beth said. "They've been coming every afternoon and I don't have the heart to turn them away. They bring cakes and casseroles for Matthew."

"He's become their new pin-up boy since you moved here," Gemma said, shaking her head as if such devotion made no sense to her. "I guess it's because they're so old he looks young to them." She looked at Beth again. "You really do look shattered. If you want to go upstairs and rest, I can watch Gwynnie. I could bring her up to you if she disturbs."

Beth smiled, grateful for the young girl's concern and common sense. "I'd like a cup of coffee to liven me up and a catch up on your news," she said. "I haven't seen you for a while, not since you started your study leave. A quiet chat will do me good. They talk a lot, but they don't include me in their conversations."

Gemma set to and washed the cups and saucers and then made them both a cup of coffee. She settled into the rocking chair, curling her long legs beneath her before bringing Beth up to date with her news. She only had to go in to college to take her exams. She was doing the last few papers. She was pinning her hopes on getting the grades she needed to study Chemistry at Warwick.

"How have the exams been so far?" Beth asked.

Gemma smiled and crossed her fingers. "I don't want to speak too soon."

"Never good to tempt fate." Beth nodded in agreement. She looked more closely at the girl, realising just how pretty she was and how oblivious she was to it. She wore her long, fair hair in a high ponytail, and her skin was glowing. She was willowy and looked stylish in her skinny jeans and baggy tee shirt. It was a low-maintenance appearance that appealed to Beth's simple tastes.

She had been impressed by Gemma's resourcefulness and tact when she got rid of the kindly women. She could see why her parents were so proud of her. "I'm so grateful for this bit of normality. You handled them so well."

"Have they been dropping in every day?" Gemma asked.

"Ever since Matthew went back to work," Beth said. "They bring us food, but they stay all afternoon and it's getting too much. We can't possibly eat everything they make, and yet they bring more each day. I think some of them are hard of hearing. They talk so loudly it makes my head spin. I'm dizzy by the time they leave."

Gemma uncurled her legs and hugged her knees to her chest and looked thoughtful for a couple of minutes. "I can come round and study here in the afternoons, if you can find me a corner," she said. "Then I can answer the door and tell them you're resting."

Beth was touched by the thoughtfulness, and so desperate for some quiet that she agreed. "If you could, I'd be grateful. Maybe they'd get the message after a couple of days, and then you wouldn't need to come," she said.

"I'd want to keep coming. I'd love to work here. The phone never stops ringing at home, now my mum works from there. She can't answer it quietly. You can hear her voice booming all over the house." She looked around the tiny sitting room. "Can you find me a space to work? I hope you have Wi-Fi. The past papers are all online."

"You can work in Matthew's study," Beth replied. "It's actually the box room upstairs, but study sounds better for a man of the cloth. It's too small to fit Gwynnie's cot and changing table in it so we've moved a table and chair in." She smiled, "Amazingly, though, we do have Wi-Fi."

Gemma didn't stay long but promised to be back on Monday at around one, assuring Beth that although she wouldn't be eating any casserole, she would take one for the team and scoff a few of the cakes stockpiled in the larder. She advised Beth to make sure Matthew kept the biddies at bay over the weekend.

"I'll tell my mum to ease up on the baking," she said with

a grin. "I'll take her latest offering back home. You clearly don't need it."

"Won't your mum be offended?"

"Of course not. I'll tell her you'll still be able to feed the five thousand without her scones and sausage rolls." Both laughed.

Gemma insisted she could see herself out.

With gratitude, Beth said goodbye and eased her feet on to the settee, settling back to rest. Baby Gwynnie slept on. Beth had longed to be a mother, and those well-meaning women had been turning what should have been magical early days into a nightmare. Gemma's offer seemed her chance to get that magic back once more. She was grateful.

Matthew was unusually ruffled when he got home. He gave her his usual hearty hug and then spent a minute gazing at Gwynnie, but she could tell he was edgy.

"What's wrong?"

At first, he said there was nothing wrong and picked up the day's mail, scanning the envelopes. Then he threw them onto the table unopened. "They've ordered me a new car. A company car." He paused while Beth absorbed the news. "What will it look like if I'm swanning about in a new car? We're supposed to spend the funds we raise on the centres."

That was typical of Matthew, she thought. He was committed to fighting poverty, and this proposed new car was bound to jar every principle he had. The charity's work rested entirely on public donations, and she knew he wanted every penny to be ploughed into that.

"I guess they got fed up with our jalopy letting you down," she said. "How many times have you been late for meetings?"

"That's not the point. The money we raise isn't for swanky cars."

"I know that, but they have to make sure you're reliable. They know you can't afford a decent car on your salary. What are they thinking of getting you?"

He paused. "A lease on a Volkswagen Golf."

"That's hardly swanky," Beth observed. "I'm not sure our rusty old Fiesta creates a good impression with your potential sponsors. And it keeps breaking down."

He huffed. "I'm still going to fight them on this. People don't donate their money to provide me with a new car."

Beth let the matter rest for the time being. She could take it up later. He covered a lot of miles every week and it would make her feel easier if he was driving a safe and reliable car.

"What's for dinner?" he asked.

"Casserole. Chicken, beef or lamb?" she asked.

"If I have another casserole, I'll go mad. That will be every day since we came home with Gwynnie."

Beth laughed, knowing there was a slight exaggeration there. However, she could see his point. The ladies had been reliably consistent but unadventurous with their cooking.

"Stuff it. Let's raid the piggy bank and order a pizza," he said. "It's the weekend. We both need a treat."

"Really, Father Matthew," she said. "A little gratitude to the old ladies' cooking would be nice."

"A little respect, wife, if you please," he said with a grin. "I'll order and then I'll get showered and changed."

She watched him go upstairs and her heart gave the little skippy beat it always did when they were together and happy. Pizza would be good, she thought, and there had been a bottle of wine in the fridge that Gemma's parents had sent over when Gwynnie was born. It would do him good, and she might even allow herself a sip or two. She hadn't tasted wine since she'd found out she was pregnant.

Pizza and a bottle of Pinot. That had been their ritual when they'd first started dating. She smiled. It hadn't really been dating, they had just spent time together. She had been a nanny, and he was the vicar of the parish she worked in. The old days had been good, and it would be nice to give the casseroles a miss and reminisce a little.

She had to admit they'd never envisaged coming so far so quickly. Matthew was fully recovered from the stabbing that had once threatened his life, and she was growing stronger each day. Gwynnie was a good baby. She was starting to be alert for short spells, but for the most part she slept and fed at regular intervals. She was sleeping better at night, settling down immediately after her feeds. Even their dog, Sasha, was house trained by then and relatively well-behaved most of the time.

As they chatted over their pizza, Beth told him how Gemma had rescued her from his admirers, explaining the plan to stop the daily visits. He agreed with her assessment of Gemma. She was a sensible, good-hearted girl, and terrifically intelligent. He said he owed her his thanks, because whilst he knew those church ladies were acting with the best of intentions, he was all too aware how overwhelming their ceaseless chatter could be.

"You've made remarkable progress since the old days," he said. "I don't want them to drive you back into your shell. They don't realise how much you need your peace and quiet."

"I still get stressed when a lot of people are talking at once," she said. "Even after all this time."

"I'll get a note put in the parish newsletter to thank everyone for their support, but I'll say we're coping now and won't need the food parcels. It will go out on Sunday. Their intrusions have got to stop. Not only that, I'm going to end up with type two diabetes if I keep eating all their cakes. We'll have to pack their stuff up for the food bank tomorrow."

"We need to save a few cakes back for Gemma. It's part of the deal."

Beth knew him well. She'd had time to think, and she was ready to respond to the car issue. He needed to see the benefits for them all, so she brought the subject up as if a thought had just occurred to her.

"VWs have a tremendous safety record," she said. "I'd be happier with Gwynnie in the back of one of those." She said no more. She hoped he would think it over and reach the right decision.

He still had plenty to tell her about his day. He had been offered premises for the first centre in the chain he was going to set up. It had been an old church hall and already had a functioning kitchen and adequate toilet facilities.

As he talked, the boyish enthusiasm crept back, and she could tell how re-energised he was. It was good to see him buzzing with ideas again. "Head Office has heard from someone who wants to sponsor the refurb."

That was good news. Beth was pleased things were falling into place.

"It's some local woman who runs a frozen ready meal factory. Alison Armstrong. High-end stuff. She supplies all the big supermarkets with fancy microwave dinners. You know, the sort of thing Tess Hargreaves used to buy."

"I think I've heard of her. The one I'm thinking of won a national business award last year. She was the first female recipient."

Matthew nodded. "That's her. I'm meeting her at HQ next week to start discussions." He grinned at Beth. "I need to get her backing. I'll do my homework and find out all about her over the weekend. Then I can schmooze her."

"You'll need to find another strategy," she said. "You're rubbish at schmoozing."

"True." They both laughed.

Matthew spent some of Saturday morning searching the internet for news of the potential sponsor.

"Read this," he said, putting the laptop on her knees. "It's fascinating."

Beth scanned the article he'd found in a Sunday Times

supplement. She learned Alison Armstrong had made the Rich 100 list that year and had won the title Entrepreneur of the Year. She was smiling out from the page, a large, confident-looking woman of late middle age with platinum hair and perfect, heavily applied makeup.

The article told how she and her mother had fled to a women's refuge to escape from her abusive father. The refuge had helped to find them a flat and a job at a local café for her mother. That was where Alison Armstrong had developed her interest in cooking, going on to catering college after leaving school. Years of work in cafés and gastropubs had led to her opening her own place, backed by her first husband.

When it became successful, she had developed the takeaway side of the business. From there, she'd moved into prepared meals to be taken away and warmed up at home. That had been such a runaway success she'd closed the café to develop it as her primary business.

Backed by her second husband, she had taken on larger premises, equipping them for meal preparation and packing. Backed by her third husband, she had taken on industrial-sized premises, got contracts with the high-end supermarkets, hired extra staff and expanded her business rapidly. Contracts had flooded in, and she now headed a sizeable empire.

"She can certainly afford to back you," Beth said, after scanning the first few paragraphs. She read on. "Oh, my goodness, she's been married three times." She read on further. "What a pity her husbands all died."

He looked over her shoulder and pointed to the last paragraph. It revealed the first husband had died suddenly from an undetected heart condition, the second had died in a motorway pile up and the third from old age.

Each one had not only backed her in her business but, when they'd died, they'd left most of their assets to her. "She's had her share of bad luck, but she knows how to put her inheritances to good use. She's a shrewd lady," he said.

"It looks as if she wants to give something back. You'll have to get her onside."

He nodded. Beth knew how much he needed to secure funds from Alison Armstrong to get the new centre running. A big investment was vital to boost the trickle that was coming in from the charity shops. She hoped this woman would be someone he could work with.

Monday was a quiet day at the cottage, thanks to Gemma. She arrived at exactly one o'clock, anxious to get to work on a Chemistry paper. She had to run downstairs to answer the door three times that afternoon. The visitors didn't bring food — the message in the newsletter had stopped that — but it hadn't been enough to keep them from calling.

She explained she was babysitting and studying while Beth rested, saying that Matthew didn't want her disturbed. They departed without argument, praising him for his thoughtfulness and saying goodbye in hushed tones.

Gemma had left at four. The house was calm and quiet when Matthew arrived home. Beth could see he was worked up. He explained he'd been so stressed by his meeting with Alison Armstrong that he had forgotten to register his protest against the order for the new car. The lease was going ahead, unopposed by him.

"It was meant to be," she said. She was secretly delighted they would have a reliable family car. "What did she do to upset you?"

"The dreadful woman groped me!"

Beth looked at him in astonishment.

"I can't work with her, no matter how much she's willing to contribute. She's a total liability." He went over to peep at his daughter, who was stretching and resettling herself in her crib and his face softened into the loving expression Beth adored.

"What happened?"

13

"We had a perfectly good meeting with the board at head office; then we left together. She got into the lift first, I followed and then turned to press the button."

"So what did she do?"

"She grabbed hold of my . . . bum, stroked it all over and then squeezed it really slowly."

"So what did you do? Did you say anything?"

"I shot into the corner, back against the wall, to get away from her. I was speechless. Can you believe she was grinning when she got out of the lift?"

He shuddered and shook his head in disbelief. "It made my flesh crawl. There's no way I can work with her."

Beth knew Matthew wasn't equipped to handle a situation like that. He would never be able to laugh or shrug it off. She could see he was hurt and angry, but she also knew the charity expected him to get the woman's financial support, which presented him with a dilemma.

She put her arms round him and pulled him close. "After you've had a shower, you can come down and cuddle Gwynnie. Focus on her whilst our dinner cooks," she said. "We can talk about it when you feel a bit calmer and have had more time to think."

She needed time to think, too. She couldn't question him further right then because he was too agitated. She thought about it as she prepared their meal. It was hard to believe a successful businesswoman could stoop so low. It was such a cheap and sleazy trick.

When he came down, she lifted Gwynnie from her crib and put her in his arms. She watched his whole body relax. He was looking at their baby and smiling at her and talking to her in his soothing, adoring way. It allowed Beth to relax a little too. They could talk about Alison Armstrong later.

When they'd eaten their meal and the baby was in bed, it was time to talk.

"You're trained to have difficult conversations," Beth said. "You're going to have to talk to her."

"You're joking. I don't want to see her again," he said.

He knew that the woman's sponsorship was crucial to the success of the first day centre, and he didn't want to create waves, but she had put him in a terrible situation.

"Then phone her. You need to get this sorted. You won't sleep with this on your mind. Have you got her number?"

He nodded. He sat in silence for a while, then stood up with determination, picked up his phone and dialled.

"Alison, it's Matthew Thomas." He left the room as he spoke.

Beth cleared the dishes from the table and washed them whilst she waited for his return. He came back, grinning broadly.

"Don't just stand there grinning," she said. "Tell me what happened."

"She said if I'd not called her this evening the deal would have been off. Thank goodness you made me call. It was a stupid test to see how far I'd go to get her money. Ridiculous!"

"A test? The stupid woman. There's nothing for you to grin about. I've never heard anything so preposterous. You could have had her locked up. She's supposed to be an intelligent businesswoman."

"She is, but she's street smart."

"That's not what I call any kind of smart," Beth said.

He poured himself a glass of water and began to tell her the story.

Alison Armstrong had explained she had lived a hard life and it made her constantly wary. She'd learned to trust no one. She said although she'd become rich, she was the same tough woman she'd always been. She had devised her clumsy plan to see how low he would stoop to secure her sponsorship. It was, she had said, a test of his integrity.

"She's the one lacking integrity. You've got plenty. You're a man of the cloth, for God's sake."

"Alison doesn't know that. She only knows me as Matthew Thomas from the charity. She said when she and her mother were desperate, our charity, Homeless Aid, as it was then, gave them the only help they got. They organized their escape to a refuge and eventually found them a flat and got work for her mother. She wants to give something back to us."

"You can't take money off a woman like that. She's shameless."

"Hear me out. As soon as she answered the phone, I told her I couldn't work with her and would be asking the board to decline her offer. She hooted with laughter, congratulated me and said I'd passed the test and we could have the money."

"You don't need to pass tests," Beth said.

"Agreed," he said. "I told her that. I told her I'd never heard of anything so stupid or humiliating."

"I'm astonished you were so blunt," she said. "I'm proud of you for being so direct. Is that it, then?"

"No," he said. "She was quick to apologise. I told her there could be no repeat of it with me or anyone else if we proceed. I explained everyone involved with us must be beyond reproach. She said that was exactly why she tested me before she signed over the money."

"And how did groping you prove it?"

"I showed I was prepared to walk away. She asked me to keep faith with her and I agreed. I'm not taking any risks, though."

"What will you do? Are you going to tell the board?"

"Not the specifics, but they'll have to carry out a full background police check anyway. Everyone involved in the project has to be screened, including sponsors."

He started grinning again and he could see it was

exasperating his wife.

"That woman groped you purely to assure herself you've got integrity. I could have told her that without her laying hands on you. She's . . . she's . . . vulgar." She frowned. 'Stop grinning. I don't think it's funny," she said.

"I know," he agreed, but Beth's indignation only increased his amusement. He snorted as he remembered Alison's closing remark. "She said I was to tell you that you're a lucky woman."

"And you can tell her she's a cheeky cow."

Matthew roared with laughter and hugged her. He was confident by then Alison was simply a rough diamond. What she'd said had assured him she was fully committed to helping establish the centre. He could see it was a cause close to her heart. It was a relief not to have lost their first major sponsor so early in the enterprise. He said he'd alert the board, in his own way, that they would be getting involved with a loose cannon who would need watching.

"It's good to know you were jealous," he said, grinning again. He ducked as she aimed a feigned blow at him. "I've never been chick-bait before."

"Don't kid yourself. She's no chick, and you're no bait. You can't go around letting strange women handle your assets," she said, finally laughing, "and she's definitely very strange."

The next day, Gemma stopped work at four and made coffee for Beth and herself. She raided the cake tin as she had promised and polished off several of the ladies' dainty little iced cakes.

They chatted about Gemma's forthcoming prom. She said she didn't have a date but was philosophical about that. Some of her friends didn't have a partner either and they were all going to share a limo and stick together. She was going shopping for a dress at the weekend with her mum, quite definite that she wasn't looking for a meringue of a dress, just something simple. She gave some hilarious descriptions of her friends' dresses.

"Did you have a prom?" she asked.

Beth pulled a face. "Yes."

"Tell me about it," Gemma said.

"It was all very traumatic. My boyfriend dumped me two days before and I was totally heartbroken. I wasn't going to go but my friends dragged me along."

"Ouch!"

"It was very ouch indeed! He was there with his new girl, and they were all over each other. I was drinking too much and laughing too loud, trying to show I didn't care when I was really in pieces."

"You were allowed to drink in those days?"

"Yes. We were all over eighteen. Things were more relaxed in those days. Anyway, back to my sorry story. The saddest boy in the year asked me to dance and tried to snog my face off. To make it worse, he had acne and bad breath."

"What did you do?"

"I gagged and ran to the toilets and threw up. Then I cried my eyes out."

"Not good," Gemma said. "But you survived."

"You have to. There's no choice." There was more to that than Gemma would ever need to know.

"What's it like being married to a priest?" Gemma asked, changing the subject. "Do you have to be religious all the time? Are there a lot of prayers and bible readings?"

There was nothing offensive in the way Gemma spoke. She was simply curious.

"You just have to be in love," Beth said. "It's that simple. Everything else works itself out. Matthew accepts how I feel."

"Wow!" Gemma was impressed. "That's so cool. I want someone who looks at me the way Matthew looks at you when he thinks no one is watching. It's not always very vicar-like. Sometimes it's positively hot. I hope I find someone who feels like that about me one day."

Beth smiled. It was refreshing to talk to Gemma. She was a curious mixture of wisdom and naivety.

She was glad of their arrangement to keep the women at bay and was relieved to hear Gemma would be coming round the next two afternoons. She was hoping to restore her equilibrium now that she was getting some peace.

It had been odd for her to look back to the end of her school days. She and Matthew had focused on her recovery from the attack, and sometimes it felt as if she had not existed before she knew him. It reminded her that she had experienced a life before it had all crashed down around her. Realising that had to be a good thing. She was more than a victim — she was a woman with her own story. She smiled. She was also a woman whose husband cast secret hot looks at her.

Matthew could tell she was feeling better as soon as he got home. She was sitting on the floor, playing with Gwynnie. It made him feel blessed when he saw them together. The baby was following the toy with her eyes as Beth moved it from side to side. He was sure he heard her give a tiny chuckle.

"How have you got on?" she asked. "Did you meet that woman?"

"Yes, we mapped out her sponsorship. She's invited us to dinner to celebrate."

Beth groaned.

"I told her it would have to wait a couple of weeks till we've got ourselves sorted. She may forget she ever asked."

"We can live in hope," Beth said, having no wish to come face to face with this person. "I hope you warned the board she needed watching."

"I did. They could see she lacked polish as soon as they met her, but they were impressed by her sincerity. I still think you'll like her," Matthew said. "She's a bit rough, but she's genuine."

It was typical of him to be ready to move on, even after such a shaky start.

"Did the coven descend again this afternoon?" he asked.

"Only two of them. Gemma worked her magic, and they went away, loving you more than ever."

He joined them on the floor, kissing them both. His world was back in harmony now he'd sorted out the Alison Armstrong issue and he'd found Beth and their baby so happy and relaxed. He was totally content with their life in the tiny little cottage. If his two girls were safe and well, he had no desire for more.

CHAPTER TWO

When Gemma stopped in after her last exam, she seemed more animated than ever. Beth assumed it was because the exam pressure was finally lifted. They talked about how that afternoon's paper had gone and how her place in the halls of residence was now confirmed. Beth began to sense there was more to her excitement than all of that.

"You keep grinning," she said. "Has finishing your exams brought you all this joy?"

"I've got a date for the prom."

"Wow," Beth replied. She could see Gemma was delighted, despite all her earlier level-headed pronouncements that it didn't bother her to go alone. "When did all this happen?"

"This afternoon. When we were going down the drive after the exam, some boys called us over. They were with this really cool guy called Janos. When they told him I'd not got a date he offered to go with me. He said it would be a crime for me to go alone. One of the boys had a spare ticket and he bought it off him right there."

Beth was cautious both by nature and through bitter experience, but she could also see how much this meant to Gemma.

"So, do you know him?"

"Not really, but some of the boys have known him for ages. Sometimes he waits in his car for them when they leave college, and sometimes he waits around for them at the gates."

"How old is he?" Beth tried to sound as if the answer was of no consequence.

"Older than the boys," Gemma said. "Twenty something, I

guess. He's really good looking. Very dark haired and myste-rious, like Heathcliff in Wuthering Heights. The boys really like him, or they wouldn't hang out with him. They say he'll be a millionaire by the time he's twenty-five."

Beth sighed silently. Where was the level-headed Gemma? An older man hanging out at college gates making friends with students sounded suspicious to her. "I guess you'll have to sort it out with your parents. Weren't you and your friends hiring a limo to get you there?"

"We still will. I'm not missing out on that. We've had it booked for ages. He said he'd meet me there."

"Well, make sure you tell your parents that's what's going to happen."

"Okay, granny Beth," Gemma replied.

"Have all your friends got dates now?" Beth knew it was time to change the subject.

"Yes. All that talk about girl power," she laughed. "They've been texting and tweeting all the available boys like mad and have managed to get themselves hooked up for the night. So much for solidarity. If it wasn't for Janos, I'd be Billy no-mates."

Beth nodded. Things really didn't change, no matter how sophisticated and self-assured Gemma's generation seemed. She hoped the girl's common sense would make her be honest with her parents.

Matthew listened to Beth's news about Gemma. She said she had been wondering about calling Gemma's mum, just to make sure she knew about this Janos.

He wasn't keen on that idea, simply because it went against his instincts to betray a confidence. "Don't do anything yet," he advised. He knew Beth was overly fearful about women's safety, but he also knew she had every reason to be cautious. "I'll be there. I'll keep an eye on her."

"Thanks. That makes me feel better."

He didn't say it, but he didn't like the idea of Gemma dating someone who regularly lurked around the college gates. He had been a governor at Gemma's college for some years and was aware there were drug problems.

That night he would be obliged to don a dinner jacket and attend the prom. "I shall circulate and smile, as usual, but I'll be looking out for trouble. It's an alcohol-free event. The college has hired reputable security people, and they know it's their job to ensure it's a drug-free event too." He was trying his best to reassure Beth.

He was an idealist, but that didn't stop him being realistic. Getting stabbed by someone he'd been trying to help had made him more cautious. He knew how to recognise trouble.

He had a lot to tell her as he got ready for the prom. He was full of optimism, because he had met the architects on site, and they said the refurbishment promised to be more straightforward than expected. He was full of praise for Alison Armstrong.

"She has a laser-sharp mind and soon vetoed any extravagance or unnecessary addition the architects wanted, yet she wasn't afraid to add on what she saw as essentials. She's insisted on a sprinkler system and a full alarm system. She's a shrewd woman. She said the place will be a magnet for vandals. She was very clear, "

Let's not make it easy for them. Anyway, you might end up with a crack head deciding to cook himself lunch. I don't want the kitchen going up in flames."

"That's great," Beth said.

"She also insisted that metal shutters should be installed. I wasn't keen on the idea because they would make the place look uninviting. Alison said the investment would reduce insurance premiums and stop windows being smashed by vandals. In the end, I could see she was right."

He had seen that day Alison Armstrong was a wise partner, and he'd found himself admiring her practical approach. She'd said she would bring the contractors from her factory refit on board as sponsors, knowing they could recoup any contribution they made through their tax returns.

"By the time the meeting had ended every decision had been finalised and the architects were able to go away to finish the plans. She had even managed to negotiate a hefty reduction in their fees before they left. I'm really glad she's come on board."

"It sounds as if she's just what you need. You've many skills, but you've not really got a killer instinct when it comes to business."

"Alison certainly has," he said. "She's fearless."

Beth had listened in amazement at the progress he had made that day, and she was glad to hear how relaxed he was about working with the woman who, only days before, had terrified him and thrown him into a panic.

She waved him off to the prom and promised not to wait up.

It was late when he returned. She was still awake, and she could tell by the way he was sighing as he undressed that he was stressed.

"I'll have to get the car to the valet service tomorrow," he said when he saw she was awake.

"Why?" Their old Fiesta hardly merited that expense. He'd used it that night, not wanting to use the new car for a non-work trip.

"I had to take a couple of lads home who were worse for wear and one of them was sick in the back. We won't be able to get rid of that smell unless I get it professionally cleaned. Thank goodness it wasn't the new car."

"I thought it was supposed to be an alcohol-free affair," she said.

"They sneaked it in and drank it in the toilets."

"Classy," she said. "Where were their parents? Why couldn't they collect them?"

"They said they'd had a drink or two and couldn't drive over to fetch them. We couldn't just put the lads in a taxi. They were absolutely out of it. They'd just about finished off a bottle of vodka."

Beth sat up. "Complete idiots! Anyway, I'm more interested in hearing about Gemma than the drunken lads."

He said she'd looked nice. Beth had wanted more detail than that, but Matthew had no interest in women's fashion. "She had a nice frock. It was long, I think, and blue."

"Did she have a good time?"

He sat on the bed beside her. "Do I smell of vomit? I suppose I ought to shower."

"You're fine."

"I think I'll just go and shower."

She knew him so well that she knew he was avoiding talking about Gemma. She curled up again. She could wait.

He was soon back, smelling of soap and toothpaste.

She snuggled up to him, enjoying the freshness of the scents.

"Tell me about Gemma."

"We have a problem," he said.

"Janos?"

He nodded, putting his arm round her. "He's trouble. He's very flash, and very smooth. He knows he's good looking and he went around as if he owned the place, leaving Gemma with her girlfriends. They weren't bothered, I don't think they stopped dancing all night."

"That doesn't sound too bad," she said.

"Beth, I know he was working the place even though he never put a foot wrong. He went round chatting to the boys, doing all that macho street greeting stuff, and then moving on to the next group."

"That doesn't sound too bad."

"It was what the teaching staff told me that worried me. They've had the police out to move him on from the college gates loads of times, but he keeps coming back. The police have searched him, but he's always been clean. They know he's dealing but they haven't been able to prove it. Apparently, this is how he sets up his deals. He arranges a meeting place, changing it each time so there's no trail."

"I wonder if Gemma knows."

"I should think it'd be hard for her not to know. Anyway, she was dancing with her friends all night, so she wasn't involved in any of that. I tried to talk to him, but he looked at me as if I was filth and slithered away. The sickening thing was, at the end of the night, when the slow dances started, he was all over her." He shook his head.

Beth could imagine the scene. "He didn't take her home, did he?"

"Thankfully, no. She went off in a taxi with her girlfriends, but that was after he'd made a meal of kissing her goodnight and handling her all over."

They fell silent for a while.

"The problem was there was nothing I could do without showing her up in front of her friends. I couldn't tell him to take his hands off her. He's a slimeball, Beth."

"So, what do we do?"

"Get our car cleaned and hope that that's the last she sees of Janos."

"She's usually really clued up. Surely she can see through him?"

"Apparently not," he said.

They both sighed. There was nothing they could do that night except put out the light and curl up to try to sleep.

Beth couldn't settle. Everything Matthew had told her

made her uneasy. She listened endlessly to the rhythmic breathing of her husband and baby and wished she too could sleep.

Gemma called in on the Monday morning to show Beth the photographs from the prom. They were mostly selfies taken with her group of friends, but there were a couple her mother had taken of her as she left the house and at the side of the limo.

Beth could see she had looked beautiful in her simple, stylish way. Gemma was still buzzing about the evening because, in her eyes, it had all been perfect.

Janos, she said, had been a sweetheart and let her enjoy dancing with her friends. He'd not crowded her but had swept in as soon as everyone had taken to the floor in couples at the end of the night.

"He's a wonderful dancer. I felt so special in is arms," she said, explaining how handsome he had looked, and how envious her friends had been.

"Do any of your girlfriends know him?" Beth asked, thinking of the college gate connection.

"Only the ones who hang around the gates with the lads after college."

Gemma showed Beth his picture. He was directing a smouldering look at the camera. His shirt collar was open, and his bow tie hung undone. It was a contrived look, as far as Beth was concerned, but he was undeniably handsome, and she could see he clearly knew it. His dark hair was immaculately styled, his face was cleanly shaved, and he had a glowing tan.

"Has he been on holiday?" Beth asked. "He's got a lovely tan."

Gemma hooted. "It's a salon job," she said. "All the cool boys get their chests waxed and then have a spray tan. Anyway, don't you think he's gorgeous?" Gemma asked.

Beth laughed. "I can see you do," she replied. "It was nice of him to partner you to the prom. Did he ask you to go out with him again?" She wanted to discover if the prom had been a once-only date.

Gemma was fussing over Gwynnie, trying to make her smile. She was pulling faces and making baby noises to tempt her to giggle. Eventually, she gave an answer. "We text a lot. He's talking about taking me to a club," she said.

"I didn't think you went clubbing."

"I don't. I've never been to one. I'll have to work on my parents to allow it, and I'll have to borrow something to wear." She grinned. "I can't go in my tracky bottoms."

"Maybe if they met Janos, they'd be happier to let you go." Beth was glad Gemma wanted her parents' approval and was hopeful her suggestion would push her into inviting him to her home.

"Beth! I can't ask him to meet my olds so soon. We've not seen each other since the prom. He'd run a mile if I invited him home. Is that what you had to do in the olden days? Did you have to take Matthew home for approval?" She laughed.

Beth smiled too, explaining that her parents lived abroad and had never met him. She left it at that. Some things were best unsaid. She had good parents but, when she'd reached eighteen and left school, she knew they were yearning for adventure. She had persuaded them it was time for them to live their life as they wished. They had taken some convincing, but she had eventually won them over. They'd started planning their odyssey the day she moved into town to start her training at the accountancy office.

She had always thought of them both as aging hippies, tormented by wanderlust and unable to settle. They had given her the first eighteen years of her life willingly, and she had no complaints. They had created a loving home and had lavished care on her. It had been Beth who had decided it was time for them to follow their dreams and roam where the spirit took them. She had no wish to share their adventure, but she didn't want to be the reason to prevent it.

It struck her at Gemma's age she had been living alone, free to do exactly as she pleased. She had none of her parents' restlessness and had settled for a quiet existence. There had been no Janos to push her off course, and she often felt that her sheltered life was why she'd crumbled so totally and completely after the attack. She pushed those thoughts away. She was a wife and mother now and all that was behind her.

Their conversation had done absolutely nothing to put Beth's mind at ease, and she was wary of turning it into an interrogation.

Gemma said she was desperate for him to arrange their night out.

"Just make sure you tell your parents if he does."

"Yes, granny Beth," Gemma laughed.

Beth hoped he would never ask.

Gemma called in the next week, and they caught up on the news. She explained she was gathering things together for her impending move to university and had started on her summer reading list.

"Have you heard any more from your prom date?"

"He texts me all the time, but we still haven't had a date yet." She said she hoped to get her parents onside before they went on a date. That sounded reassuringly slow and sensible, so Beth let the subject rest.

After they'd had coffee Gemma suddenly suggested they take Gwynnie for a walk. Beth was surprised but she jumped at the chance. She needed some fresh air and wanted to keep building up her stamina. She would be glad of the company on a stroll.

It was a beautiful day, so they headed for the park. From there Gemma suggested they take the footpath along the brook. Sasha trotted along beside them, and apart from having to adjust the sunshade to keep the baby out of the sun, Beth was able to relax as she found she could manage the steady pace without pain.

"Look," Gemma said suddenly. "There's Janos." She pointed to a figure stretched out beneath a tree.

He had heard her voice and he sat up slowly, waving them over to him.

Beth was no fool. She realised at once that this was no co-incidence. Gemma had taken her along as an alibi and was trying to maintain the pretence.

"Come and say hello," she said. Beth followed her reluctantly. "Janos, this is my friend, Beth."

He stood and stretched his hand towards her, his lips smiling in a way that had neither warmth nor interest. Beth ignored him and turned to Gemma.

"I'll be off," she said. "I'm sorry, I can't serve my purpose. Gwynnie and I won't be your alibi. If you two want to meet, be adult about it. Come clean to your parents, Gemma."

Gemma's face fell—clearly, she was astonished her subterfuge had been detected.

Beth turned the buggy round abruptly, unable to get involved in the plan Gemma had devised. She was not there to provide an alibi or give her approval to their relationship. She had counselled Gemma to be open with her parents, and she meant it. She decided Gemma was old enough to stand by her own choices without ensnaring herself and her baby in her schemes.

She set off at a pace that, if she was honest, was too quick for her stamina, but she was angry and wanted to get home. She could see Gemma had wanted to tell her parents that she'd been on a walk with Beth and Gwynnie, and they had happened to come across Janos.

Gemma was trying to make her developing relationship with him seem unremarkable to her parents and had made Beth part of her plan. She had no doubt that Gemma had expected her to be totally charmed by Janos and able to recommend him to her parents when she next saw them.

As she walked, Beth wondered if Gemma understood the dangers that Janos represented. She had thought the girl was being naïve, but now she had doubts. Gemma wouldn't be concocting schemes if she thought he was on the level. She knew Matthew thought Gemma must know about Janos selling drugs. She found she agreed with him. Surely Gemma must have heard about the deals he was setting up at the college gates day after day.

She would be glad to talk to Matthew.

He listened to her story. "That's so disappointing," he said. "I didn't think Gemma would be manipulative."

"I'm glad you understand. I was scared you'd think I was over-reacting."

"Funnily enough, I heard from her father this afternoon. I'd approached him for his support for the centre, and he got straight back to me. He wants us to go for dinner. I said I'd check with you first," he said. "You were so alarmed by Alison's invitation."

"That's different. I know Edward and Diana and I'm comfortable with them, but I'm not leaving Gwynnie with a babysitter. We've never left her before, and I don't know anyone in the village well enough to ask. You'll have to ask if we can take her along."

"I'll call them to check," he said, picking up his phone and going into the kitchen.

He came back after a few minutes. "Diana answered. She insisted on Gemma babysitting so we could have our first night out together. I couldn't very well say no."

Beth sighed. "Up until today I'd have had no concerns."

"You've always said how good Gemma is with Gwynnie. It will be fine. Anyway, we can find out if they know about

Janos yet. It will be easier with Gemma out of the way," he said. "I've been putting out feelers about him with my police contact. Nothing's come back yet, so that's reassuring."

"Let's hope it stays that way and we're worrying about nothing."

Gemma visited a couple of days after the disastrous walk. Beth could see she was anxious to remain on good terms with her.

"I'm sorry I set you up the other day," she said. "I wanted you to see how nice he is, so you'd be able to tell my mum and dad. I really want them to like him, and it seemed a good idea at the time. They really trust you."

"It's never a good idea to try to fool someone," Beth said. "I suppose you've seen him since then?"

Gemma nodded. "A couple of times. I've still not told my parents."

"You really must," Beth said. "If he's as nice as you say he is, there's no reason not to tell them."

"I suppose so. You won't tell them when you go for dinner?" she asked. "I'd rather tell them myself."

"I won't lie for you," Beth replied, evading her question. She had a tight bond with Gemma's mother. Her loyalty to Diana meant the knowledge she had about Gemma and Janos weighed heavily. She changed the subject. "Have you got everything you need for university?"

"Two of most things," Gemma laughed. "You know what my mum's like. Oh, by the way, she said she'd like me to babysit when you go over."

"I was thinking of taking Gwynnie with us," Beth said, trying to get out of the arrangement as tactfully as she could. She had never been happy at the idea.

"There's no need to do that. She'll be tucked up in bed by the time you leave, and I could call you if I was worried.

You'd be back in a jiffy. We only live a couple of streets away."

"I'm not sure I'm ready," Beth said. "I've never left her with anyone, not even Matthew."

"I'll glue my eyes to the baby monitor, and I'll guard her with my life."

"It's a big responsibility."

"And I'm very responsible, despite dragging you off to meet Janos. I have said how sorry I am."

"Can I let you know?" Beth said.

Gemma nodded.

She talked it over again with Matthew. He didn't share her reluctance and persuaded her it would look rude to Edward and Diana if they turned down Gemma's offer and turned up with the baby in tow.

She had fed Gwynnie and put her into her cot just as Gemma arrived. She waited till the baby nestled down before switching the monitor on and going downstairs.

She laboured over the instructions, still wary about leaving Gemma in charge. She made her promise to call if she had the slightest concern, saying she would return at once if there was a problem.

"I think you've made everything really clear," Matthew said. "Shiny, crystally, sparklingly clear and bright. In fact, if we don't go now, it will be time to come back."

"Don't forget to help yourself to coffee and cake," Beth said. She turned back as she reached the front door. "Don't have the TV on too loud. You might not hear the monitor."

"I promise."

"Beth," Matthew said. "Come on."

It was not only the first time they had left their baby, but it was also their first outing as a couple since her birth. Matthew seemed glad of the opportunity, but she would have preferred to stay at home, keeping a watchful eye on the monitor.

She knew there would be plenty of time in the future to go out as a couple.

Her common sense told her Matthew needed to firm up Edward's support for the day centre, so she had to accept it was something that had to be done.

Edward and Diana Hooper were extremely well off. Their home exuded money and privilege in a stylish yet understated way. Beth was sure the cars in the drive were worth more than Matthew would be able to earn in years. They handled their elevated situation with such grace and charm she always felt at ease in their company.

That evening they were so welcoming she relaxed a little and allowed her inner panic at leaving Gwynnie with Gemma in charge to subside a little.

Edward's support for the day centre proved easy to confirm. He owned a bakery and a chain of bread shops and was perfectly happy to supply his unsold stock to the centre. He was even prepared to get it delivered early each morning.

"My accountant's working on the tax advantages I can get. I think it's win, win," he said, shaking Matthew's hand.

She was relieved for Matthew. A similar arrangement had worked well at his previous centre. He was always tense when trying to secure help from sponsors, so she knew he'd be relieved it was settled.

Diana had brought the food through, and they moved to the table. Their conversation strayed into more domestic matters. The Hoopers exhausted the topic of baby Gwynnie. Their questions about her sleep patterns, her smiling and her cooing had all finally been answered and so it seemed natural for Beth to enquire about Gemma. She asked how her plans for university were going.

"Don't talk to me about that!" Diana said with dramatic effect, laying down her knife and fork.

Beth and Matthew exchanged glances.

"She's talking about taking a year out," Edward said.

"She was looking forward to it the last time we talked," Beth said. "It was only a couple of days ago. When did she change her mind?"

"Yesterday," Diana said. "She came home and said she was thinking about deferring."

There was an awkward pause. They continued to eat and then, as if she could contain herself no longer, Diana said they were wondering if there wasn't some boy behind it all.

Beth knew the importance of respecting confidences, but Diana needed to know Gemma was potentially at risk. This was her chance. She could see Matthew was pondering how to proceed, so she spoke first, hoping to pave the way for him.

"She bumped into a man when we took Gwynnie for a walk," she used the word *man* deliberately but kept her tone casual. "He seemed pleased to see her."

"That might be the chap she danced a lot with at the prom," Matthew added.

She knew he too was being careful in what he was saying.

He frowned. "The teachers were a bit uneasy about him."

Edward put his knife and fork down, alarm on his face. "Why?"

"He hangs around outside the gates at the end of college, apparently. They've asked the police to move him away a few times. He does move, but he makes a point of letting them know he has every right to be there. They were surprised he turned up at the prom, and they didn't like the way he worked his way round the room."

Beth could see the couple were reading between the lines.

"He did nothing out of order," he added, "so there was nothing they could do. They kept their eyes on him, but he gave them no reason to ask him to leave."

"I don't like the sound of him. But it was a private event," Edward said. "Surely they could have just told him to leave?"

"He had a ticket. He was there as a guest," Matthew

replied.

Beth shot him a knowing look. It was clear Gemma had still said nothing to her parents.

An unease descended. Beth knew they had achieved the best result they could, since they had no hard evidence against Janos. They had alerted Gemma's parents to potential problems, and they had protected her as far as they could.

Dessert was over and a cloud of anxiety had descended over Edward and Diana.

"I hope you won't think we're rude if we make a move. I want to get back to Gwynnie," Beth said. She knew Edward and Diana would want to talk about what they'd heard.

"Beth feels as if she's missing a limb when Gwynnie's not close by," Matthew said.

"I do feel odd," she said. "It's the first time we've ever been apart."

"I remember that feeling, but she'll be fine with Gem," Diana said. "She adores that baby. She would have called if there'd been a problem."

Beth left the goodbyes to Matthew, knowing he excelled at pleasantries. He said all the right things about the meal and wine before they left. She could sense Gemma's parents were unsettled by what they had heard and was glad they had some awareness of what was troubling her and Matthew.

She went upstairs to Gwynnie's room as soon as they got home. She held her own breath until she tuned into the sleeping baby's rhythmic breathing. Her anxiety left her. She felt whole again now they were reunited. She allowed herself a couple of minutes to enjoy the sight of her little girl fast asleep, flat on her back, with her head on one side. Thankful she was safe and sound, Beth headed downstairs.

She was surprised by Matthew's sharp tone as she went into the kitchen.

"Have you been smoking dope?" he asked Gemma.

He had let Sasha out. The unmistakeable sweet smell had started to seep in through the open back door. She saw him step outside and sniff the air to confirm his suspicions.

She knew by the way colour rose to Gemma's face he had caught her out.

The girl nodded, looking awkward and embarrassed.

"Has he been here?" he asked.

Initially Beth thought Gemma was going to deny it, but, eventually, she nodded. It was then she noticed the two tell-tale glasses upturned on the draining board. "You've been drinking." It was a statement, not a question.

She nodded again. "Just a glass of wine. You said I could help myself and there was a bottle in the fridge."

"I said you could help yourself to coffee and cake. I didn't invite you to open a bottle of wine." She could see the empty bottle in the bin. "And finish it."

"We left you in charge of our baby," Matthew said. "It was the first time we've ever left her. How could you, Gemma?"

"We only smoked a bit of weed." Her voice tailed off.

Beth felt stricken. She had believed Gemma thought enough of Gwynnie to behave responsibly and her disappointment was overwhelming.

"Has he been near my baby?" she asked.

Gemma shook her head, protesting that she'd never have let that happen. "Of course not. He didn't go upstairs, not even to the toilet. I was looking after Gwynnie properly."

Beth was beyond exasperation. "You weren't or you wouldn't have been smoking dope and drinking. God knows what else you got up to."

Gemma was now in tears, saying repeatedly how sorry she was.

Beth was not inclined to listen, stunned by her irresponsibility.

"I'm taking you home," Matthew said. "Get your things."

Beth was grateful he was taking control.

"I drove here. I can take myself home," she said.

"Don't be ridiculous." Matthew picked up his keys. "You've been drinking and smoking dope."

"Don't tell my mum and dad," she begged. "Please don't tell them. They'll go mad."

"Again, don't be ridiculous." His voice was like ice and Beth could see Gemma was shocked by his tone.

"Please don't be like this," Gemma pleaded.

"How do you expect me to be? You put our baby at risk and let a drug dealer into our home." Matthew turned his back on her.

"Beth?" she said. "I just didn't think."

Beth felt anger overwhelming her. "You mean, you didn't think we'd find out."

Gemma grabbed her bag and followed Matthew meekly to the door.

"Beth, I'm so sorry," she repeated. "Please don't stop me seeing Gwynnie."

"Just go," Beth said, closing the door behind them.

She went straight upstairs and deliberately, but guiltily, made a noise with the door handle as she went into the nursery. Gwynnie stirred at the sound, just as Beth had hoped she would. She scooped her up and settled into the nursing chair, breathing in the heavenly scent of the baby's freshly washed baby hair.

She was more angry with herself than she was with Gemma. She had never wanted her to babysit, but it had never entered her head that the girl would bring that man into their home, let alone smoke dope and drink whilst she was caring for Gwynnie. She was furious with herself for going against her own judgment.

She had to wait until her breathing calmed before she fed Gwynnie, who was making sleepy attempts to latch on to her. She couldn't bring herself to put her down after the feed. She waited until Matthew returned, knowing he too would want a few minutes with their baby in his arms before they tried to settle for the night.

She was right. Matthew took her and brushed his lips across her soft downy hair, closing his eyes.

He told her what had happened at the Hoopers as they got ready for bed.

"They were shocked," he said. "I told them Janos had been here and they'd smoked a joint and polished off a bottle of wine. I went on a bit too much really, but Gemma had totally betrayed our trust. As far as I'm concerned, she put Gwynnie at risk."

"She did," she said. "What did the Hoopers say?"

"What could they say? They were sorry, obviously, but, beyond that, there was nothing they could add to make it any better. I've no idea what happened next. I couldn't leave fast enough. I wanted to get back here. I truly wish I'd spoken to them the night of the prom."

"And I regret leaving Gwynnie with her. And I should have told Diana about the walk. So much for giving Gemma the benefit of the doubt."

It was late the next afternoon when Gemma arrived to collect her car. Gwynnie had only just settled to sleep so, when Beth opened the door, she had a finger to her lips.

Gemma nodded and followed her through to the sitting room.

Beth was still angry, but she said she was glad she had called when she could have simply picked up her car and disappeared. She could see Gemma was stressed and tearful, so she assumed that things had been difficult at home.

"I don't know how to tell you how sorry I am," she said.

"I don't want to hear it unless you mean it," Beth said.

"Of course I mean it," she said. "I should never have asked

him to come."

"We agree on that. And I should never have trusted you."

"I know and I'm sorry, but I need your advice."

Beth didn't understand why Gemma wanted to confide in her when she'd made it absolutely clear she was angry.

"I really need to talk to you," Gemma said. "My parents have read me the riot act, and I know I deserved it. They've banned me from seeing him again."

"You can't blame them for that. He's not a good influence," Beth said.

"Please listen to me. I can't talk to my friends."

"Why not?"

"One of them would blab. That's what it's like in our group. There are no secrets between us, but secrets are never kept. At least one wouldn't be able to resist sharing the news and then it ends up on social media. They all do it at some point. I'm not prepared to go viral on Facebook or be the subject of the latest Twitter storm."

"What was it you wanted to say?" Beth asked, feeling awkward in the silence between them and wanting the girl to say what she had to say and then leave.

Gemma looked relieved at the invitation to speak. She explained that she wanted to apologise again for what had happened the previous night and that she loved little Gwynnie and would never have let her come to harm.

"You put yourself in a position where you might not have been able to prevent it," Beth said. "I know nothing happened, but you were lucky. We were lucky. We thought we could trust you."

"You can."

"We won't be putting that to the test again."

"I don't blame you. I really let you down," she said.

"What else did you want to say?"

Tears start streaming from Gemma's eyes. Ever practical, Beth reached for the box of tissues and passed it to her.

"I'm going to hurt a lot of people," she sobbed," and I just can't help it."

It sounded ominous, as if the girl had reached a huge decision. "I'll put the kettle on," Beth said, going into the kitchen to allow Gemma time to pull herself together.

She had composed herself by the time Beth returned with the coffee. She wiped her eyes.

"Better?" Beth asked.

Gemma nodded.

"You'd better tell me." Beth sat down in her armchair.

She explained her dilemma. Her parents had forbidden her from seeing Janos, but she had no intention of obeying them.

Beth listened in silence.

"Beth, he's in my head. He's all I think about. I'm not being a rebellious teenager or a defiant daughter. I love him, and I am going to keep seeing him. I have to keep seeing him. Being apart from him would kill me."

"I doubt you'd actually die," Beth said.

"You don't know what it's like when we're alone together. It's all happened so quickly. It's overwhelming. The . . . sexy . . . things he does to me, the things we do, the way he makes me feel. I can't give that up. I can't live without him. I'm not going to stop seeing him, but that means disobeying my parents. Then that will be it. They'll throw me out. They've made it absolutely clear they'll never forgive me. And the rest of the family will side with them."

"You've obviously seen more of him than you've led me believe. And you've obviously been alone together. Have you been to his home?"

"No. We've been in his car," Gemma said.

Beth wondered if she realised how sleazy that sounded. "And you're definitely taking a year out?"

Gemma nodded. "I can't be in Warwick when I feel like this. I may never go at all if we stay together, which I'm sure we will."

"Drink your coffee," Beth said. She thought for a few minutes before speaking. "I can't imagine your parents would want you to leave home. Are you sure he'd let you move in with him if you did?"

"When they say I can't see him they're forcing me to leave home. Don't you see that? He loves me. I know he'd let me move in. He loves me." Gemma was getting exasperated. "Look!"

She pulled the waistband of her joggers down to reveal the tattoo on her thigh.

It was in elegant script, *Property of Janos Farkas.*

It both shocked and repulsed Beth. There was no way she could see that as a statement of undying love. As far as she was concerned, it was all about the power he had over her.

"You see," Gemma said. "It's real. He wants it to last."

"The tattoo certainly will," Beth said, "unless you have it removed by laser." She shuddered, remembering the word Jackson had carved on her. This tattoo seemed equally as demeaning.

"I don't want it removed. It's better than a diamond ring."

"Cheaper, too. Did he have your name tattooed on him?"

"He had a horse tattooed on his shoulder. He said that's my spirit animal."

Beth sighed. She couldn't believe Gemma had abandoned her common sense so completely. She knew she was heading for a conversation she'd have preferred not to have, but she was terrified Gemma was putting herself at risk.

"I've no idea how far things have gone between you," she said. "Pretty far, from what you said. I know you won't thank me for asking you, but I need to make sure you're looking after yourself. Is Janos using a condom?"

Gemma looked at her for what seemed an age before replying. "He will be. We've not actually had sex yet. We've just done stuff. Obviously, he wants me to go on the pill, but until I do, he'll have to use one. He doesn't want me getting pregnant."

"That's not all I was worried about. He's a lot older than you, and I'm sure he's had plenty of girlfriends. I don't doubt he wants you on the pill, but I want you to take responsibility for yourself." Beth breathed deeply. "I was in a situation where I had to be tested for STIs, HIV and Hep B, so I know what I'm talking about. Unprotected sex brings risks. You might be willing to trust Janos with your life, but you still have to protect yourself. He can't vouch for all the women he's been with."

"I wish I could have had this conversation with my mum," she said. "All she could say was I was never to see him again. At least you're being realistic about what's happening. You can see I'm not going to give him up."

"You can't blame her. She's only just found out you've been drinking and doing drugs with him. That all came as a shock."

"We only smoked a bit of weed." Gemma was still defensive about that. "But I can see your point. It must have been a lot to take in."

They continued to talk. Gemma made it clear she didn't want to sever the ties with home, but Janos was non-negotiable. She had arrived with a few things stashed into a backpack and was intending to spend her first night at his flat, giving her parents a clear signal of her intent.

"I want you to talk to your mum again before you take off for the night. She'll be frantic with worry," Beth said. "I'm not sure she'll be ready to talk it through, let alone agree to what you want, but you've got to give her the chance. You're not even sure he'll want you to move in with him."

Gemma looked at Beth as if she was crazy. "We're in love," she said, exasperated. "Of course he'll let me move in."

Beth picked up her phone. "I'm calling your mum and I'm going to tell her you need to talk to her. Will you go straight over?"

"Yes, but I'm still going to stay with Janos tonight."

Beth made the call to Diana. There was no more she could do.

Matthew listened to Beth's account and assured her she had handled it as well as anyone could have. He was a realist, and he knew how easy it was for men like Janos to turn young girls' heads. He was more interested in keeping her safe than wasting time supporting bans that could never be enforced.

"You've got her to speak to Diana, and you've drilled it into her about safe sex. No one could have done more."

"I'm not so sure about that. I wanted to tell her to stop being stupid and accept that he's no good."

"She wouldn't have listened."

"I don't know how you used to do it, day after day," Beth said. "No wonder trying to sort everyone's problems out by yourself nearly drove you crazy. I know I did my best today, but what if I got it wrong?"

"You did all you could. It's better than doing nothing. By the sounds of it, you were brilliant."

He had finally heard from his friend in the police force and knew what he had heard would not reassure her. Janos had been on their radar for months and they had assembled a clear profile of his various activities. His friend described him as a vicious, small-time lowlife with a big ego. The police knew he was dealing to college kids and running a backstreet protection racket. They had no hard evidence and could do nothing because no one was prepared to press charges against him. His record remained squeaky clean.

"You've got to tell the Hoopers," she said. "They mustn't throw Gemma out. He'll drag her down. They have to keep building bridges."

"You're right, but I really don't look forward to it. I wish he'd just get out of our lives for good."

CHAPTER THREE

Gemma looked round at Janos' flat, and her heart sank. It was not what he had led her to expect. It was, in the kindest terms, a dump. She tried to excuse it, reasoning that he lived alone and that, underneath the mess, there were signs of good taste. It crossed her mind that it would take her weeks to clean it if she ever lived there permanently. Her fanciful images of their perfect home together took a hefty knock.

He had ordered takeaway and had already started the wine. He cleared the black leather sofa and coffee table of clutter by sweeping it into a pile with his arm and dumping it on the floor. Gemma's stomach churned as a multitude of sticky rings clagged with dust and cigarette ash appeared once the glass top was exposed. They were soon covered with the newly arrived takeaway trays, and she forced the image from her mind.

They ate, they drank and then, as the alcohol took hold, he poured out his story. She listened with rapt attention, hanging on every word. She was too much in love to examine what he said with any objectivity.

He explained his parents had come to live in England to seek a better life for their family when he was three. They had struggled to provide a decent home for him and his two sisters. "I watched my dad work himself to death and I swore right then that wasn't going to happen to me. I was smart, see, and I kept my wits about me as I grew up. I watched and I learned the ways of the streets. School had nothing to teach me."

"Those days must have been tough," Gemma said, trying to imagine the hardships his family had faced.

"They were. My dad died when I was thirteen. He was a complete loser by then, totally worn out and broke. I had to help my mum make ends meet, so I started doing errands for the thieves and fences who were working our area."

She shook her head in sadness. "That's awful," she said. "I suppose you had no choice."

"We needed the money, and I was learning stuff. Anyway, all that's behind me. I'm an entrepreneur now. I've got others to do my errands. They call me an up-and-coming business-man round here. They say I'll have made my first million by the time I'm twenty-five."

She already knew the boys at college said that. She was swallowing every word he said, seeing him as a street urchin who had clawed his way up from the gutter.

"I'm trying to build my portfolio," he said. Even the word *portfolio* impressed her. It sounded high powered. "It's not that easy, though. For the time being, I'm dabbling in any-thing that turns a quick profit because I need the cash. It's a high-risk strategy, but I make sure I leave no traces. If anyone I use is stupid enough to get caught, they know better than to point the finger at me." He paused.

She knew he was watching her, waiting for a reaction so she nodded, wanting him to see she understood.

"All this is temporary. I need to build up capital, and I don't have a rich daddy to bankroll me."

She didn't register the possible implication. She was still swallowing every word.

"I need capital to expand."

"Is there no way you can make money without getting in-volved in all this?" she asked. "I hate to think you're putting yourself in danger."

"I can handle myself. I learnt that on the streets. But you're my future. You've got the class to make people take us

46

seriously. With you in the office, we'll be on our way up. You'll be booking appointments and meeting and greeting my clients. You'll make us look like a classy outfit. I'll be able to clinch more deals than ever before."

"I'm going to work for you?" she asked. "Really?"

"We're the dream team, you and me. Together we can get things moving." He slipped his arm round her. "I need you, baby. You already know you can't leave me to go to Warwick. You'd miss me too much."

Gemma remembered how easily his touch could excite her, how crazy she was about him and how she thought about him night and day. She shivered with delight. She saw she was part of his long-term plans. The shady things he did would soon be a thing of the past as his business grew.

"I don't fancy telling my parents I'm going to work for you, not after they tried to ban me from seeing you."

"You're a grown up now. You can do what you want. We must stay together, baby. I have plans for you. We're going to make my business grow." He explained he ran a small-scale security business by selling his services to several small independent backstreet shops. "These shopkeepers make their living by trading from dawn to the early hours, selling everything they can cram into their premises. Many of them are sitting targets. Some lowlifes just want to steal booze and cigarettes off them, but there's some racist scum who want to drive them out of business just for the hell of it. My hired hands keep them safe. They are happy to pay for that safety," he said. "Plus, I get them to install security cameras and alarms, which my guys fit. They claim what they pay me against taxes. I send them monthly invoices and they get peace of mind. It's win, win!"

"That's wonderful," Gemma said.

"I do my bit," he said. "I own a couple of flats as well."

"You're into property too?" She was even more impressed.

"I let one to a family, but I let two illegal immigrants have the other at a reduced rate. They're twins from Romania, terrified of the immigration people finding them. They work the streets." He said they had no choice, they had to make their living from prostitution. "It's sad, they're lovely girls. They know being twins is good for business, it brings in the punters. I know what it's like to have to make hard choices." He shook his head and paused.

Gemma was impressed by how thoughtful he was being to those girls.

"It's tough for them. They can't get regular work. I make sure my boys keep an eye on them."

"You're amazing," she said. "They must be glad you're there to keep them safe." She was in love and her heart swelled at the thought her man was so full of kindness. *In his own way, he's just like Matthew. He's trying to help the needy.*

"You know I deal?" he asked.

She nodded.

"Like I said, it's only temporary," he said. He belched from deep within his stomach. "Excuse me, baby, it's that second bottle. I think it's loosened my tongue, but I can trust you, can't I, baby?"

"Of course."

"I rely on the fat pockets of the kids at places like your old college because it's easy pickings."

Gemma knew what he said was true. The students bought willingly and could easily afford to pay. They would have got their gear from someone else if he stopped trading. *Better they buy from Janos, who has two sisters and an ailing mother to support, than from some villain.* This elevated him above the ranks of other dealers. *After all, what he is doing is only temporary.*

"The kids at college are impressed. They think the gear you provide is good and they think you're cool."

"So that little innocent at the prom with the *butter wouldn't melt* thing was all an act?" he laughed. "You knew all along what I do?"

48

"Sort of," she said. "I'd heard talk. But I'd never indulged until that night we babysat."

"The night we got down and got a bit dirty?" He leered at her. "Anyway, tell me some more about what those dumb kids think."

"They drool over your designer gear and your tattoos. They love the BMW and its blacked-out windows." She shivered as she remembered the encounters they'd had in it and the way he'd made her feel.

"Getting the right gear for the kids means mixing with the guys involved in drug running across county lines." He paused.

She knew he was looking at her for her reaction.

"I can't show any sign of weakness to them. They'd slit me wide open if I gave them any reason."

"You must be careful. I don't like to think you're in danger." She had read all about those gangs.

"I can hold my own with anyone. I told you, I learned on the streets," he said. "And you needn't be scared. You'll always be safe with me by your side. These men may look down on me, but I'll show them one day. I pick up the deals they pass over." He laughed. "There are rules. There's a hierarchy, and it has to be respected, but I'm working my way up that ladder. They just don't realise how fast I can climb."

"But when your business takes off, you'll be able to leave all that behind," she said, putting her hopes in his mouth.

"That's the plan." He filled his glass and sipped it thoughtfully before admitting to Gemma that he despised the kids who bought their gear from him. He said they knew nothing of the struggles he and his family had faced because everything came so easily to them.

"They've never had to buy cheap plastic trainers from the market and stick fake stickers on to pimp them up. They've never had to wear their cousins' stinking cast off clothes for school." He stopped for a second. "Actually," he said, "they never stank. My mother scrubbed them clean—but she still had to patch and darn them. Those patches and darns marked me out as one of the have nots. Everyone knew me and my sisters were on free school meals, another stigma we had to bear thanks to our useless father. I've waited for the day I could get some real money in my pocket. I'm going to give my family the life he never could."

"I'd love to meet your mother and your sisters," she said. "They must be so proud of you."

"I could never take you to my real home. I would be too ashamed," he said.

"There would be no need," she said. "I wouldn't mind if they lived in a shack."

"As I said, I would be too ashamed," he replied. "The kids I despise have never been hungry. If they want a car, then their daddy buys it. They've always had plenty of cash in their pockets."

She knew what he was saying was true. She knew it was true of her too, but assumed she was exempt from disdain. *He respects me. He wouldn't want me to see the poverty his family live in.*

"But we're in this together. You're smart, you know people. You're good looking. With a bit of guidance, you could be stunning. The two of us, baby, are going to the very top. We're going to make waves. You'll open the doors that are closed to me."

"Sounds great," she said.

"And now I'm going to finish your education. You're already a dirty little baby," he said. "It's time to complete your corruption."

She giggled. She did not need to analyse his words. She had known, after all they'd been doing, it was only a matter of time before they had sex. She accepted without question that it would be that night.

He lowered his voice to a whisper. "I can already make you

groan with pleasure, but we still have a long way to go, baby. I'll have you screaming with delight tonight."

It was inevitable she would surrender her body to him. She had already surrendered her heart, and with it, the common sense and objectivity she'd once been proud of. She drank in every word he said. She was sure he loved her. He was going to make it as a businessman and abandon all his shady dealings and she was going to be at his side.

She tried to shut out the odour of the stale sheets as they lay together, nor did she examine any of the rest of her squalid surroundings. Her eyes were closed where Janos was involved.

Janos left just before she got up, saying he had to go to a meeting. He promised he would call her later. She spent an age in the shower, thinking about the pleasures of the previous night that had been repeated that morning. This, she thought, was the start of something wonderful.

He'd asked her to go home to broker an improved understanding with her parents, saying family was what mattered above all things so she must smooth things over with them.

She knew she'd been totally stubborn and uncompromising with her parents, so she wasn't looking forward to it but, if that was what he wanted, she would do it for him. She was clear about her terms as she headed off to negotiate with her parents. She would not be going to university, there were to be no more objections to her seeing Janos and the freedom to flit between home and his flat as she pleased was essential.

She didn't question Janos' reluctance to have her move in permanently. He'd explained he would be happier if she was safe at home with her parents when he was away on business. With all this in her mind, she arrived home, confident in her new womanhood, determined to make them accept her chosen direction.

Her mother was alone, expecting her father to return from his meeting any minute. Gemma hoped she could talk to her mother and escape before he got home. She knew her mother would be easier to persuade.

"Mum, we need to sort this," she said. "Janos insisted I come and visit you. He wants us all to get on."

She made it clear she was never going to give him up and was prepared to move in with him permanently if necessary. She emphasised how much she loved them and how she didn't want to have to walk away, but said they had to accept Janos as a non-negotiable fixture in her life.

"Mum, I love him. He wants us to make a future together. I'm going to work in his office, so I definitely won't be going to university. I'm sorry I'm shattering your dreams, but I can't live without him."

"But you're not actually moving in with him?" Diana asked, afraid of the answer.

"He doesn't want me to. He believes in family and thinks I should build bridges and stay here some of the time. He'll know I'm safe when he's away on business." She was watching her mother's face, trying to read her reaction. "I'll be staying over with him sometimes, of course, but I'd like to live here with you and Dad."

"You want the best of both worlds?"

She shrank at the harshness in her mother's tone. It made her see, if only for a second, what a lot she was asking of her parents. "Mum, I've fallen in love, and I want you and Dad to get to know Janos. You'll really like him, and you'll see he really loves me."

"You're asking a lot. He's not exactly squeaky clean, is he?"

"He's trying to get his business going. He wants to leave all the bad stuff behind, and I'm going to help him. He's told me everything."

"You've obviously believed every word he's said," her mother said.

"Of course, I have."

Diana sighed. "I'll talk to your dad."

"But can I come home tonight?"

"It's your home, Gemma. Make of that what you like."

Edward had arrived back by then. He caught the end of their conversation as he went into the kitchen.

"Have you given in to her demands? Are we going to do everything she says?" Edward asked.

Gemma flinched. She had never heard him refer to her as *she* before.

"I've listened and said I would talk to you about it." She glanced at her daughter, who was looking awkward. "I also told her this will always be her home."

"Ours too, Diana. It's not just her hotel," he said.

His mobile rang at that moment, and he took the call. "I've got to go," he said to Diana. "There's a fire at the Welby shop. The fire service is there now." He grabbed his keys. "Phone Matthew and ask him to meet me there."

He had left before Diana had chance to ask any questions. She phoned Matthew and gave him the message.

"That didn't go too well," Gemma remarked. "I didn't know Dad could be like that." She sighed. "I hope there's not too much damage at the shop, though I don't know what good a priest can do at a fire."

"They're friends," Diana replied. "Your dad relies on Matthew."

Gemma went up to her room. For the first time in her life, she didn't feel totally welcome in her own home.

Matthew didn't hesitate to respond to Diana's call and headed to Edward's shop. The five-mile drive took him into Welby, a sleepy commuter village.

The fire was out by the time he got there. It had been a low-impact blaze. No one was hurt, because it was early closing day and the staff had already locked up and gone home.

The fire officer told them a few lit fireworks had been posted through the letter box. They had ignited the tiers of wicker bread baskets stashed by the door. These had burnt away and there was a degree of smoke damage, but the fire had not spread much beyond the doorway.

"Kids. Local vandals, I expect," the chief fire officer said. The shop had no CCTV and there were no cameras set up on the small village's main street.

Edward Hooper said nothing to contradict him and thanked him for preventing the fire spreading. He waited for them all to leave before he was able to tell Matthew he was scared. Matthew wanted to know why, but by that time the contractors had arrived to shutter the doors the fire brigade had smashed to gain entry.

"We can't talk here," he said, nodding towards the men. "Anyway, it stinks of smoke." He nodded in the direction of the village pub. "The stench is sticking in my throat. I need a drink. Let's go to the pub, and I'll tell you what I know." He told the contractors where to drop off the keys when they finished. The two walked over the road.

"It could have been worse," Matthew said, trying to break Edward's silence.

"Could it? Wait until we're in the pub and I'll tell you what happened today."

Edward brought the drinks to their table and sat down with a sigh. "That man, that Janos, came to see me today."

Matthew was astonished. "What did he want?"

"To throw his weight about. He strolled into my office as bold as you like and ordered me to sit down. Then he emptied his pockets. He laid a spoon, a lighter, a length of surgical hose and a small plastic packet on my desk. He made a meal of it, holding each one to the light and fingering it before he put it down. He took his time to make sure the line of stuff was dead straight and equally spaced. He was going for maximum impact."

"Heroin paraphernalia?" Matthew asked.

"I assume so. *Just a little gift for Gemma that I keep by me. I want you to look at it and listen to my proposition. It will help to focus your mind on my offer*, he said. I was scared out of my mind."

"My God," Matthew said. "That's terrifying."

"He was enjoying the moment and he knew he was completely in charge. His offer was simple. He would protect my five retail outlets and the bakery itself in return for a premium to be paid on the first of each month. He'd ensure they all stayed safe. Any default in payment would mean Gemma would get her gift. There would be no turning back for her. She'd be desperate for more."

Matthew could see Edward reeling as he told the story. Matthew's stomach lurched. It took him some time to reply.

"Gemma's no fool," he said. "She won't be blinded by a piece of dirt like him."

"She already is," he said. "He passed me his mobile. They had sex last night and the bastard filmed it. He said *Here's your little girl losing her virginity*. Matthew, I literally retched when I saw the first few frames. I threw it on to the desk, I couldn't look."

"He's . . . vile." Adequate words were beyond Matthew at that point.

"*Temper, temper*, he said. *She's already developed a taste for deviancy that has exceeded my expectations. You'll see when you watch your movie.* He picked up his mobile and smirked, looking at that blasted video. It was still playing. I could hear them, Matthew, I could hear them. I didn't look, but I couldn't close my ears." He wiped tears from his eyes.

Matthew placed a hand on his shoulder.

"He said, *Believe me, if I can get her to do all that so soon, I can easily persuade her into a little chemical experimentation.*

Remember, she's already tried dope at the vicar's cosy cottage. He was gloating as he pocketed the paraphernalia, staring at me as he fingered each item before he put it away. He's a sadistic bastard, Matthew. I could have killed him with my bare hands right then. He sniggered at me before he left. *You have my terms, daddy dear,* he said. *I expect an invitation to a family dinner within twenty-four hours to show you've accepted my terms. I mean every word. One second's delay to my invitation and my home movie goes viral on every social media platform you can think of, and your baby girl gets her present.*"

"My God, that's awful. I don't know how you kept yourself together."

"I watched him saunter from the office. I put my head in my hands. I didn't know what to do. I felt sick to think of him touching my daughter. My common sense told me to call the police, but my heart told me not to. You'd already told me Gemma had been smoking dope and I was sure his threat to get her hooked on heroin was real. The thought of my beautiful girl being abused by that man and turned into an addict was enough to stop me making the call. He sent me the video the minute he'd left."

Matthew sighed. "What an impossible position. What does Diana know?"

"Nothing. I don't want her to. I went straight home after that, but Gem was there, throwing her weight about. She was adamant she was going to do as she liked. I hadn't had chance to say a word when the call came about the fire."

"My instincts tell me you should go straight to the police. Get him locked up, then Gemma will be safe."

"My head agrees. But my heart won't let me. They might not arrest him straight away. He could get bail. He could post that video. That would destroy Gemma. He could pump her full of heroin." He stifled a sob. "And I can't tell Diana any of this. It would kill her. And you can't tell Beth."

They were interrupted by the contractors returning

Edward's key.

Matthew went to the bar for more drinks. His heart felt weighed down. He hated the thought of keeping secrets from Beth, but he was also worried for his friend.

"I honestly don't know what to do," Edward admitted when Matthew returned. "I'd like to drag her away from him, lock her in her room and stop him ever coming near her, but that isn't possible. She really believes she's in love, and he's convinced her that he loves her. She believes every word he says. I'd like to murder him, slowly and painfully," Edward said.

As they were talking, Edward's phone pinged. It was a text from Janos. *Did Daddy enjoy his video? Shall I be giving Gemma her present or am I coming to dinner? The clock is ticking.*

"Sick bastard," Edward said, showing the message to Matthew.

They sat in silence, contemplating the dilemma Janos had created.

"Would that text and the video be enough to convince the police to lock him up?" Edward asked, thinking aloud.

"I'm sorry. I can't answer that. I wish I could. You need to go to the police and ask them."

"I can't put Gemma at risk," Edward concluded. He prepared a text. *We'll be inviting you for dinner.* He showed the message to Matthew. "What choice do I have?"

"None that I can see if you won't involve the police." He told Edward what he'd learned from his friend in the police force, making the man's concern grow. "I can put you in touch with him, off the record, if you won't press charges," he suggested. "Maybe you could work something out with him."

"I'll think about it. Remember, Diana's better off not knowing any of this, so don't mention it." he said. "She wouldn't cope."

Matthew nodded. "Beth wouldn't either," he said. He had worked hard to build up her confidence after the attack that had nearly destroyed her, and he didn't want that undone. He sighed heavily. "But I don't like deceiving her."

"I think we're actually protecting them both from a lot of anxiety," Edward replied. "I'm going to send the text." He picked up his phone, "though it doesn't feel right."

Matthew nodded. He knew exactly what Edward meant.

Beth was stunned by Gemma's appearance the next time she visited. She had been transformed into exactly the woman Janos wanted her to be. Her fair hair had been bleached, layered and was hanging in soft waves.

She was wearing false lashes and her brows had been groomed to perfection. She had had a spray tan that made her whitened teeth look alarmingly bright. Her fingernails were talon-like and painted crimson. She had ditched her vertiginous high heels at the front door, revealing matching crimson toenails. She sashayed her way to the rocking chair in her clinging cream dress. It was too tight for her normal, confident gait. It took her a while to position herself on the seat.

"You look . . . different," Beth said. She was unsure Gemma would be able to hold Gwynnie for their customary cuddle with her fiendishly long nails.

Gemma smiled, but it was not her old, good-natured grin. It was self-conscious, showing Beth she was not yet at ease in her new image.

"Janos has been spoiling me," she explained.

"So I see. Those nails will make horse riding a challenge," she said. She knew how much Gemma loved her horse and prided herself on her skills as a horsewoman.

"I've asked my dad to sell Silverado," she said. "I'm so busy in the office, and I have to look good for the company image. Janos wants me to spend all my spare time with him, I just don't get to the stables anymore. It's sad, but it's for the best."

Beth sighed. This was one more sign that the old Gemma was disappearing.

"This beauty stuff has been really exciting, though the Brazilian hurt like mad." She laughed. "I don't recommend you try it, though Janos insists on it for me."

Beth could see Gemma was out to impress her and had no idea she was achieving the opposite result.

"I don't suppose Matthew is as fussy about such things."

"Coffee?" Beth asked, changing the subject, too amused to take offence. "I'm afraid we're out of Prosecco." She was joking, but it took Gemma a couple of seconds to realise and laugh.

Over their coffee, Gemma told Beth her news. She said she'd been amazed when her parents had invited Janos over for dinner. She said he'd made a real effort, and had taken chocolates, very expensive wine, and flowers.

"Did your parents like him?" Beth asked.

"Hard to tell," Gemma was honest enough to admit her doubts. "They were polite and made him welcome. That itself was quite a result."

"Are you living with him now?"

Gemma shook her head. "Janos says it's important to respect family, so he likes me to stay at home quite a bit to please my parents. I've moved a bit of my basic stuff into his flat for when I stay over, but there isn't room to move much in. It's a bit of a man cave, to be honest."

Nothing she was saying reassured Beth, but she could see Gemma's confidence in her lover was secure. Gemma didn't seem to think it odd he didn't want her to move in with him.

"Have you met his family yet?"

"His mother and two sisters live in Leicester. He still says he'd be ashamed for me to visit them. I guess their house isn't up to much. I keep telling him it doesn't matter to me, and I wouldn't mind a bit, but he insists he'd be too ashamed."

Beth looked again at the new Gemma and knew, in her

heart, it wasn't his home he would be ashamed of. He wouldn't want them seeing him with the type of girl he associated with. She was sure his family would have loved the old, homely Gemma.

She went on to talk about her role in his business, explaining he'd just opened a small office in the back of a shop he provided security for. She said the trader was letting him use it rent free. She said he'd started importing cheap trinkets from China and was moving them on to a string of market traders. "Janos knows it's tat, but it's turning over good profits. He wants us to go more up-market as soon as we can. He thinks I'll come in useful when we do. He's keen to scale back on his more dubious activities, but he needs the money to move ahead."

She said she answered the phone, took orders, arranged deliveries and saw to the paperwork. She explained a lot of paperwork came from the invoices he sent out for his security business, saying it felt odd to be sending one to her father. She assured Beth she'd got her dad a generous discount.

"I didn't know your dad needed security."

"Neither did he, till the fire. Still, Janos has sorted everything. There's been no trouble since."

"There was no trouble before, was there?" Beth asked, suddenly connecting Janos with the fire at Edward's office. Gemma didn't seem to see any link.

She's given up everything for him. She really believes he's going to change. She's no idea she's helping him run a protection racket.

"It's good he's planning to get everything above board. I hope he succeeds." Beth was grateful to have thought of something positive to say. It alarmed her to see the way Gemma seemed to accept his shady dealings.

Beth was glad to be able to talk everything over with Matthew that evening. She described Gemma's transformation into synthetic glamour and went on to tell him of their conversation and of her suspicions.

"I didn't want to tell you about how he'd blackmailed Edward," he said, "but I can see you've worked it out. I'm sorry I kept it from you, but it was to protect you from knowing what Gemma's got herself involved in." He told her what he knew, apologising again for keeping it quiet.

"Stupid, stupid girl," Beth said. "She thinks he loves her."

Matthew nodded. "Edward Hooper wants to keep her safe. At any price. He's in touch with my contact in the police force, but, as far as he can see, his hands are tied. Janos has had him sign a contract for security services. It's all official, signed and sealed. It would never stand up in court as a protection racket."

"And Gemma sends out the invoices," Beth added, "thinking she's got her dad a generous discount."

"That's the story Diana believes too."

Beth shuddered. "I just pray Gemma sees through him soon."

"That's about all we can do," he said. "He's got Edward Hooper over a barrel with the contracts he's signed. They're watertight. He's got the video as collateral, and the threat of getting Gemma into hard drugs." He sighed. "Anyway, that's enough of Janos and his poison. Let's change the subject. My dad called me today. They're back home. He wants to know when we could visit. They're dying to meet you and see Gwynnie. I told him it would be a while before we could go over. I explained you were going into hospital next week."

"Did you tell him why?" She was going to have plastic surgery to remove the scarring on her chest.

Matthew shook his head. "They still don't know anything about what happened to you or how we met. To be honest, with what my sister told me about mum's odd behaviour, I don't think now's the time."

Beth nodded. She knew he was worried about his mother. Matthew's parents had been on an extended visit to New

Zealand to visit Bronwen, Matthew's sister, and her calls had alerted them to his mother's odd and occasionally aggressive behaviour.

"Did you ask your dad how your mum is?"

"He said he's sure she'll be fine now that she's home. He said she's just a bit disoriented by all the travelling they've done. He thinks she'll sort herself out now she's back in their own home."

Beth frowned. They knew his mother was showing signs of dementia, and Matthew had promised his sister he'd check on things when they got back. "I'm sorry you can't go straight away. I know it will worry you to death, and your dad's clearly in denial."

"Who can blame him? But please don't worry. You and Gwynnie come first. I'll go as soon as I think you'll be okay on your own."

Chapter Four

Beth, knowing Matthew was worried, offered to postpone her surgery so he could visit his parents. He told her he wouldn't hear of it.

"I don't want Gwynnie to ever see the word *Whore* on your flesh, let alone ask why it's there. I want it gone for good. Your recovery will never be complete whilst you carry that scar," he said.

She was relieved that was how he felt, but she was expected to be in hospital for two days and would take a couple of weeks to recover. It presented her with a dilemma. She knew Matthew wanted to be there for her and Gwynnie, but she also knew, although he never said a word, he was under pressure at work. The refurbishment of the centre was nearly complete, and he was needed on site more and more.

Their friend, Josie, came to the rescue as soon as Beth mentioned the problem. She offered to stay with them for as long as she was needed. She said the company would do her good and she would be glad to be useful once more.

Beth knew Josie must be lonely, although she always appeared cheerful. Her husband, Sidney, had died shortly after she had retired, and her family had moved away.

She explained she would have to share Gwynnie's room, but Josie said that made it even better. She said she was looking forward to being part of a family again.

Josie was standing on the pavement beside her suitcase when Matthew pulled up to collect her.

"It was as if she couldn't wait to get away," he had said to Beth. "I'd expected to have to go in to pick up her suitcases. She said she couldn't wait to start looking after Gwynnie, so that was why she was waiting outside."

The surgery went well, and Beth was soon back at their cottage, sore but happy. Once the dressings came off, she no longer had to avoid looking at herself in the mirror. The wounds weren't great to see, but at least the dreaded word had gone. She finally had her wish. Gwynnie would never see the scars that had haunted her for so long.

They had decided to keep the surgery quiet, with only Josie and the Hoopers knowing. They were not ashamed of what was happening, but neither of them wanted to open it up for gossip. They also wanted to prevent the visits of the women of the parish, delivering their gifts of casseroles and cakes.

Josie took over completely, leaving Matthew free to go to work and visit the hospital. When Beth was discharged, she could see Josie had everything running smoothly and had Gwynnie completely under her spell. She watched her amuse the baby when she needed entertainment and soothe her when she needed comfort. It was a relief, because she knew it would be days before she was able to lift her own child again.

It was lovely to have Josie around. The older woman knew how to help without taking over, and Beth's recovery was smoother than she and Matthew had dared hope.

It had been a long day. Gwynnie was teething and had been unsettled all day. She had finally gone to sleep in Beth's arms. Josie, having spent the day comforting the fractious child, was keen to put her feet up and watch the soaps on television. Beth was tired but content now the baby was finally settled. Matthew was working late that evening, so Josie had plated up a meal ready for warming up when he got back. Both women were glad of the peace and quiet.

They were startled by a knock on the door.

"What now?" Josie said, wearily raising herself from the rocking chair and trudging to the door.

Beth rocked the baby gently, making sure she didn't disturb.

It was Gemma, armed with a hugely expensive bouquet of flowers. "I heard you'd been in hospital," she said. "I called to make sure you're okay."

"I am," Beth said. "Josie's been looking after me."

"I thought these might cheer you up," she said, taking the flowers to the kitchen and dumping them in the sink. Beth thanked her, astonished at the extravagant flowers. The old Gemma would have raided the garden for a few random blooms and bought chocolates, expecting to eat most of them as they talked. Beth missed that girl.

The old Gemma would not have been wearing white skin-tight jeans teamed with red stilettoes. Beth was hoping the heels would not pierce through the threadbare carpet. Nor, she thought, would she have been heavily caked in make-up and reeking of expensive perfume.

"I had a brilliant idea as I was driving over." She sat herself carefully on the rocking chair, constrained by her tight trousers, oblivious that she had taken Josie's seat. "I'm going to ask Janos to get involved with Matthew's new centre. I know they need sponsors. It's so obvious. They're so alike, always trying their best for people."

Beth could see the enthusiasm in the girl's face and her heart sank. Janos was the last person she wanted at Matthew's centre, and the thought that they were alike in their philanthropy was ludicrous.

"He's been marvellous working with my dad. There's been no trouble at all since he took over his security, so I was thinking he might provide it at the centre. You know he wants to build up a good reputation. I'm going to ask him tonight."

There was no trouble until he got involved, Beth thought. "Please don't bother. They've got all that sorted," she said out loud. She knew Alison Armstrong had insisted on shutters and alarms being fitted.

"I'm going to ask him anyway," Gemma said. "He's always trying to help people. He had such a terrible childhood. Did I tell you about the Romanian girls, and all those poor shop keepers he helps keep safe? I did, didn't I? There's bound to be something he can do to help. Didn't Matthew get stabbed at the last centre he worked at? Security is Janos' speciality."

Beth was taken aback at the casual way Gemma had asked. The mention of it had turned her blood to ice. She was not prepared to talk about it. Neither did she want Janos to muscle in on Matthew's project. "His parents struggled for years to keep him and his sister fed and clothed when his dad was out of work. I think that's why he's so passionate about his centre."

"Exactly! They're so alike deep down. It makes perfect sense for Janos to get involved with the centre. And just think of all the contacts he could make with the other sponsors."

"Please don't ask him," Beth said. In a panic, she searched desperately for reasons to stop her. "He's got all those expansion plans going on and needs to get some money together. I know Matthew has security under control." It was a heart-felt plea. She knew he would turn any offer Janos made down, but, when he did, she feared a backlash.

"I'll think over what you've said," Gemma replied, "but I'm pretty sure it's a good idea."

And I'm certain it isn't. Beth shuddered.

Gemma didn't stay long, explaining she had to get back as Janos had booked a table. They were going to wine and dine a potential client. "Janos wants me to schmooze him," she said.

Beth watched her leave, wondering exactly what schmoozing clients entailed and reflecting that the girl had never

66

looked at Gwynnie once or asked after her. A few weeks before, she would have scooped her from her arms as soon as she arrived. That made her feel sad.

Gemma was changing fast, and Beth was more concerned for her than ever. The thought of Janos getting involved with the centre terrified her. She hoped she'd convinced Gemma to let the matter drop.

"I worry about that girl," Josie remarked. "She seems to have lost her way these last few weeks. There's such a pretty face under all that make-up muck, and those clothes make her look like a tart."

"She's a lovely girl deep down. But you're right, she's a bit lost right now. She thinks she's in love."

Josie nodded. "She's not the first to be led up the garden path. That girl's mistaken *you know what* for true love." She gave the knowing, womanly-wise shake of her head that always made Beth smile.

As usual, Josie is correct. Gemma's mistaken Janos' lust as love.

Matthew had a lot on his mind as he drove to the head office the next day. The shadow of Janos hung over him. He wanted to forewarn the charity's chief of the potential danger he represented, should he offer his sponsorship. He'd warned Alison about the possibility of an undesirable approach the previous evening.

He was determined to do everything he could to keep Janos out of the centre. He was hoping Gemma had done as Beth advised and said nothing to him.

Those hopes were dashed when he received a call later that afternoon to say that Janos had approached head office with a written offer to provide security personnel. He was relieved that a letter was already in the post to thank him and explain the necessary arrangements were already in place.

He slept soundly that night, glad everything had been

handled with tact.

It was an important day, and he could have done without the detour to the printers to collect advertising posters. He and Alison were due to sign off on the building work before the final redecoration started and they had to check the snagging had been completed satisfactorily.

As soon as he got to the centre, he could see Alison was worked up. Her face was flushed, and she was breathing more rapidly than usual.

"What's wrong?"

"Come into the office," she said. "I'll tell you there." She turned to the huge man standing beside her. "It's okay, Ivan. You can stay out here."

She closed the office door and turned to face him, eyes blazing with anger. "That little scrote you warned me about turned up here this morning. He tried to do a number on me, saying he was going to take over security."

Her words tumbled out. Janos had arrived without warning, walking around the place as if he owned it. She'd known at once who he was because of Matthew's warning.

"He said he was going to make sure one of his men was in attendance during opening hours to provide security. I said there must be a misunderstanding as security had already been arranged and his offer had been declined." She paused for a moment.

That's not the sort of security you'll need. You wouldn't want this place going up in flames, would you? She had his accent perfectly as she repeated his words. "He had a lighter in his hand and he kept lighting it and blowing it out. Then put his face within inches of mine and said *Accidents happen*. His breath stank."

Matthew put his head in his hands. This was exactly what he had tried to avert. "He obviously hasn't received the letter from head office yet," he said. "What did you do? Did he threaten you?"

"I'd pressed the nearest panic button the moment I realised who he was. Ivan came immediately and stood beside me, arms folded across his chest, doing his man-mountain look. It had the desired effect. The scumbag backed off a few inches. He'd been right in my face. I told him Ivan is my head of security."

"I'm so sorry, Alison. He's dangerous man."

"Don't waste your sympathy. I can look after myself. I gave his balls a mighty squeeze and told him to bugger off. I also pointed out Ivan is partial to pretty young boys, and he obligingly took a couple of steps towards him. You should have seen him run." She managed to laugh despite her stress. "Poor Ivan. That was naughty of me. He's got six kids, he hasn't got time for hobbies."

Matthew couldn't see the humour at that moment. "I hope to God you haven't made yourself an enemy. He's dangerous."

"Sunshine, I have a long line of enemies, believe me. Most of them are a lot scarier than that little turd."

"You mustn't underestimate how dangerous he is, Alison. I told you, he torched Edward Hooper's shop." He needed to ensure she understood the gravity of threat Janos represented.

"The centre's fine. We have alarms linked to the police station and the fire station. We have shutters, we have sprinklers, we have personal alarms for the staff, and we have my people here until we get funds to pay for a security presence. I pointed all this out to him."

"I really hope you're right," he said. "I don't want you or this place in any danger."

"You worry too much," she said. Her anger had faded, he could see she was ready to act in her usual brazen way. "Have you seen the size of Ivan?" she laughed. Changing the subject she said, "Anyway, it's time you and your missus came to me for that meal."

"Not until Beth's feeling better," he replied.

"Always some excuse," she retorted.

Gemma made an unexpected visit to the cottage later that afternoon. She bought no flowers on this occasion. She was seething and had driven over from the office.

Beth offered coffee but Gemma was not interested.

"What the hell is Matthew playing at?" she demanded, not even willing to accept the invitation to sit down.

"I'm sorry?"

"Turning down Janos' help. You know how good he's been for my dad's business, and he was offering our services free of charge."

Beth knew his help had been turned down but knew none of the specific details.

"I have never known him so angry," she said. "That Armstrong woman assaulted him after she'd insulted him. She crossed the line. He says he'll make her pay, and believe me, he means it."

"Gemma, you need to talk to Matthew if you have an issue. He doesn't bring the centre's business back here. This is our home. Surely you can see threatening this woman is not a good way to persuade Matthew to change his mind."

"Yes, right, but it's okay for her to threaten him?"

Beth could hear the fury in the girl's voice.

"I thought he'd understand how keen Janos is to do the right thing and give something back. They're so alike. They both want to do good."

Beth sighed. It was time to speak up. "Gemma, you know Janos deals drugs. Matthew can't have him anywhere near the centre. Use your head."

"How can we turn a corner with the business if no one gives him a chance? Matthew's a hypocrite. A sanctimonious hypocrite. You can tell him from me that woman he's working with is a nasty piece of work. You should see the bruises she left on Janos. He's not going to let it go. He wants revenge."

Beth looked at Josie and saw she was itching to fly to Matthew's defence. She had to speak to keep her silent. "I think you should go, Gemma. We'll never agree on this. Whilst Janos is dealing there can never be a role for him at the centre," she said. "I don't know what Alison Armstrong has done to him, but you must see that centre has to be drug free."

"You're just as bad as them," Gemma said. "I thought you would give him a chance. You'd better let them know this isn't finished as far as Janos is concerned." She left, banging the door behind her.

"That girl's lost her mind" Josie said.

Beth nodded. "She lost it when she lost her heart," she said. "I'll have to tell Matthew what she said. I hope there's not going to be any trouble."

CHAPTER FIVE

Beth and Matthew eventually went to Alison's for dinner, leaving their baby in Josie's care.

They were both impressed when they pulled up in front of the huge electric gates. They opened immediately, sweeping apart silently and smoothly. Her home came into full view as they moved forwards, an imposing manor house in pristine condition.

"Phew! She's even better off than I thought," Matthew said. The tyres made a crunching noise as they made contact with the gravel. There was an old gatehouse to their left, with children playing on the lawn. "I think Ivan lives there," he said.

"Ivan?"

"Her security manager. She says he's got six children."

"That's a very nice house. She must rate him to let him live there. It must be worth a fortune."

"It's not as nice as this one," he said, pulling up in front of the main entrance. "This is magnificent."

Alison appeared at the front door and welcomed them. "I should have thought. If I had, I'd have sent Ivan to pick you up. You could have both enjoyed a drink."

"Apparently, I'm going to be allowed to have a tipple. Beth's going to drive me home." Matthew hugged the woman with an ease that astonished his wife.

She was taking in the appearance of this woman she had heard so much about. Matthew had been scant on his description. Alison Armstrong was so much more impressive than the old press photographs she'd seen. She doubted he would ever have been able to describe her adequately.

She was certainly glamorous, in her own way, and well-groomed. She wasn't tall, but she was broad and imposing. Amply proportioned, Beth decided. Her generously endowed bosom was showcased by a low-cut dress. Her hair was platinum and lustrous, her long nails were a glorious shade of red, and her make-up was heavily but immaculately applied. Wafts of Chanel No. 5 invaded Beth's nostrils as Alison hugged her and bade her welcome.

Beth felt dowdy and underdressed in her faithful floral tea dress, which hung softly to her ankles and revealed her well-worn ballet pumps. She had put on a touch of makeup, but she now doubted it was even discernible.

"Come in, come in," Alison said, ushering them in.

The house was decorated and furnished to Alison's glamorous and glitzy taste. It created an immediate impact on Beth and Matthew.

"Wow," he said.

"Come through," she led them through to a sitting room. "My last husband let me go wild. When he finally saw it, he said it was a cross between a tart's boudoir and Liberace's mansion. He loved it."

"I see what he meant," Matthew said, looking round.

There was so much glitz and glamour around Beth was temporarily fazed as her eyes took it all in.

"Sit down," she said. "Don't worry, Saint Matthew. It isn't the sacrilege it looks. I put all his antique stuff into safe storage and the original features are intact behind the glitz. It can all go back to how it was when I pop my clogs and pass it on to his undeserving kids." She laughed. "His horrible offspring don't know any of that, snotty little buggers. They think they're getting this gin palace. Serves them right. They'd turned their back on their father years before I met him."

Although Beth was overwhelmed by the intensity of the presence of this woman, she found her strangely endearing.

"Something smells nice," Matthew said sniffing.

"It's me, darling. It's Chanel," she said.

"No. I meant dinner."

"There's proper food cooking. I may make my money doing fancy microwave stuff for the idle rich, but I cook real food here. I wasn't sure if you'd prefer beef or lamb, so I've done them both. I popped a chicken breast in a few minutes ago," she said to Beth, "in case you're on a light diet."

"I have been," Beth said, "but it smells so good I think I could eat it all."

"That's good. You look as if you need building up." She said it in such a pleasant way it caused Beth no concern. She had decided she liked this straight-talking woman.

Alison chattered on through dinner. She had made the best soup Beth had ever tasted, followed by roast meat and vegetables. The atmosphere around her table was relaxed and Beth was surprised to find she was enjoying herself. It felt good. She had been dreading this meeting. However, she had not quite grown accustomed to the extent of the woman's bluntness.

"What's it like being married to a saint?" she asked.

Matthew squirmed. "Alison!" he said.

"I mean it, Beth. He's the nearest thing to a saint I've ever come across. I've heard all about the fuss he made when the board wanted to provide him with a car. They're still talking about it. And he's turned down a raise."

"It's wonderful," Beth said loyally, hiding her astonishment he'd turned down a raise without telling her.

"Well, I know he likes his sack cloth and ashes," she said, "but what's he actually like in the sack?"

"Alison!" Matthew said once again.

She laughed her bosom-heaving, throaty laugh. "You can take the girl out of the gutter, but you can't take the gutter out of the girl."

Matthew blushed but, for some reason, Beth found it

funny. "Actually, he's pretty spectacular," she said. She surprised herself with her answer and immediately blushed as red as her husband. She had only been drinking elderflower cordial and had no excuse for her extraordinary reply.

"Thank you for the compliment," he said, easing his collar self-consciously," but can we please change the subject?"

That was not difficult with Alison in full flow. Conversation streamed forth.

"I can't remember eating that much, ever," Beth said, putting down her knife and fork.

"You've only pecked away like a little bird. You need pudding." She left the room and returned with a trolley laden with home-made desserts.

"Beth might not want pudding, but I do," Matthew said.

"At last, our saint reveals a secret vice. A sweet tooth." She laughed. "Mind you, Matthew, if pudding's your only vice, it's nothing to worry about."

Beth instinctively went to clear away the dishes from the main course, but Alison shook her head. She cleared the table with astonishing dexterity. "The benefits of running a café for years," she said. "Table clearing is one of my many talents."

"So I see," said Beth, as Alison stacked their plates on her extended arm.

After dessert and coffee, Alison insisted on serving Matthew a brandy, saying she was going to give Beth the grand tour. Beth was sufficiently relaxed to follow her without protest.

"I wanted a word," Alison said. "One of the things I like about Matthew is the way he speaks about you and your little girl. He obviously adores you."

"That's nice of you to say."

"It's not nice of me. I'm telling the truth." She opened the door to her room and led Beth in. It was a riot of pink and silver glamour. "Sit down with me a second." She sat on the bed and patted the space by her side. Beth obeyed, overawed by the opulence and femininity. Every surface in the room glittered, and as she sat on the bed, she felt herself sinking into its excesses of extravagant draperies. It was as if the bed's throws and furs were enshrouding her in clouds of pink and white.

"It's so . . . pretty." She had no adequate word to offer. It reminded her of a real-life Princess Barbie bedroom. It was miles wide of her taste, but it clearly suited this extraordinary woman.

"We're not here to look at the décor," she said with a smile, "though it is sumptuous." She stroked the fabrics lovingly. "I do my homework. There are no skeletons in Matthew's cupboards. He's as straight as a die, and I did test him, as I'm sure you know. That's why I can support the centre. I also understand, from a few things he's let slip, you've been through it."

Beth's eyes widened. Her heart quickened. She did not want to dig up her past, and she couldn't imagine Matthew passing on the full details.

"Don't worry. He was discreet when I asked about your recent hospital stay, but I gathered you were having the scars from an attack removed."

Suddenly uncomfortable, Beth went to stand but Alison laid a restraining hand on her lap.

"I don't talk about it," Beth said.

"Neither does he, and I really rate him for that, but he does forget he's got a wife and child when he's turning down cars and pay rises. I just wanted to tell you not to let him forget you're the one who has to live in the real world and pay your way whilst he's busy crusading."

Beth looked at Alison intently, unsure of what she meant.

"I mean he shouldn't make his family live like church mice, just because he's embraced poverty."

"That's blunt," Beth said," and we're not quite that poor."

"That's just me. I wouldn't say it if I weren't concerned. I just wanted to warn you not to let him get too carried away with his philanthropy. You and your daughter matter, as well as his beloved centres."

Beth looked at her quizzically.

"You can't live on love and fresh air, no matter how spectacular he is. Don't be afraid to remind him. I could see you had no idea he'd turned down a pay rise, and I'm sure you could have done with that extra money. Now, let's go down and join Matthew before he thinks we've got lost."

As they waited for Ivan to operate the electric gates, they both looked at the black waters of the river directly ahead of them. Although it was twinkling in their headlights it still looked menacing.

"Be careful as you turn out, Beth," he said. "The river's very close and there are no barriers."

"Yes," Beth was biting her lip as she made the manoeuvre. No streetlights aided her as she turned sharply on to the narrow road. The waters turned to inky darkness as their lights focused on the narrow road. "Good job you're not driving. Alison certainly plied you with alcohol."

He smiled, then looked harder at their surroundings. "That river's very close to the road and the bank's really steep. It looks dangerous. There should be some lights. There's an accident waiting to happen here."

Matthew headed straight round to Alison's office in a panic. She had called and asked him to go straight over. He had no idea what the urgency was.

It was only his second visit there. Despite his concern, he was impressed once more by the high-tech processing plant she had created. Its twenty second century minimalist futurism had no connection with the pink and silver fantasy palace she had created for herself.

His anxiety for her faded as soon as he saw her. She was

not fazed, but she was angry. Her cheeks were flushed, and her eyes flashed as she spoke.

"He's been here," she said.

"Thank God you're safe," he said. "What happened?"

"The easiest way is to let you watch the security video," she said, loading the footage on her screen and turning it so they could both see it. "I saw I'd got an eleven o'clock appointment on my schedule. I didn't recognise the name of the company, so I checked with my secretary. She said it was a potential new customer, wanting to discuss a contract. I carried on with my paperwork totally unconcerned." She sighed heavily. "I was astonished when my secretary showed Janos Farkas in."

"What did you do? You must have been scared."

"I flicked the alarm switch and the video recording switch. Ivan was here within a minute. He came in silently, closed the door and stood in front of it with his arms folded across his chest."

"Thank God for that," Matthew said.

"You'd better watch the rest for yourself," she said. "It's beyond belief. Seeing it is better than me describing what happened."

Matthew watched the arrogant way Janos had staggered in and was amazed to see him turn his back on Ivan and settle, uninvited, into a chair.

"I've come to offer you a deal."

"I don't want you, your business or your deals."

Matthew saw Alison had shown no fear.

"You will, Mrs. Armstrong, once you hear the deal. Imagine one of your employees were to smuggle in some . . . let's call it . . . bacteria. Suppose they were to introduce it to the manufacturing process. Imagine an outbreak of E. coli or listeria being traced back to your factory."

"Alison, this is terrible," Matthew said, before turning his full attention back to the screen.

He heard Alison say, "Have you forgotten Ivan already? I choose who we do business with, and he keeps undesirables away."

He could see Janos was not fazed. "Forget Ivan. Imagine how easy it would be for me to get to one of your staff. One with gambling debts, say, or just bad money troubles. A simple arrangement with me would mean that poor employee, who was so desperate for cash, would take my money and smuggle in the bacteria. In they'd come, they'd slip that extra ingredient into one of your dishes, and bingo, your reputation would disappear down the toilet along with your five stars for hygiene. Your devoted customers would go down with food poisoning."

"Alison, it gets worse!" Matthew ran his fingers distractedly through his hair. "What have I dragged you into?"

He watched the screen in awe, witnessing Alison taking command.

"You've got some balls coming in here making threats, though I seem to recall they were particularly tiny. See that up there?" She pointed to the camera. "That's a recording device. I have filmed this whole conversation." He saw Janos look upwards and take in the fish-eyed device he had noticed in the corner.

He was proud of the way Alison had taken control and watched Janos's body language change. His shoulders sagged. His face lost its bullying sneer.

"That recording can go to the police right now, or I can keep a copy with the company lawyer. If you go anywhere near me, any one of my staff, the centre I support or anyone I know, that goes straight to the police. Ivan will show you out, having first taken you through the screening process everyone entering or leaving the food processing area is contractually obliged to accept. That should convince you not to approach my staff."

Matthew saw one last glimmer of defiance in Janos. "You

bitch," he heard him say.

He saw the woman's strength of character once again. "True," she had said. "But I'm a rich bitch and a clever bitch too. Fuck off, Mr. Farkas. Goodbye and don't come back. I hope you enjoy your strip search. I know Ivan will."

Matthew watched the fury resurface in Janos. "You'll pay for this," he said, his rat-face twisting up in anger.

He was impressed to see Alison remained unmoved. "Very probably," he heard her say, "but I won't be paying you. You're out of your league, little boy."

He watched Ivan jerk his head towards the door as he opened it. Janos had stood without protest and left the room. Ivan had followed him and closed the door behind them

Alison switched off the recording.

"He's unbelievable," Matthew said. "I don't know where you got your courage from. You must have been shaking inside."

"I was, but I'm fine now I've had time to think. I'm sure our security here is too tight for a small-time operator like him to penetrate. I'm worried about the centre, though. He could easily get at a volunteer or one of the ancillary staff. They won't be subject to the security procedures my staff have to go through."

"We both know he wants to deal from there. It has to be his only motive."

She nodded.

"Thank goodness you filmed it," Matthew said. "Despite what you said, you've got to hand that recording to the police. Let's get him out of circulation. He must be shaking in his boots in case they pick him up."

"I won't be doing that. I like to keep something in reserve. Collateral." She looked directly at Matthew. "People like me don't go running to the police. We fight our own battles."

Matthew understood her reasoning, but he did not agree with it. "Alison, I don't just worry about the centre, I worry about you. You have made a very dangerous enemy even more angry. Please go to the police."

"I planned to make him angry."

"It's *his* plans that worry me. The centre is going to be a drug free zone, no matter what. That and your safety are my chief concerns. You need to be responsible and go to the police."

"I am being responsible. Have you met Ivan?" She smiled. "You think he's menacing? You should see his foot soldiers. They're animals. I'm going to put the heavy mob in the centre for as long as we think we need them. That's what I call being responsible."

Matthew was ill at ease with Alison's decision. The more he tried to persuade her to go to the police, the more stubborn she became.

He appreciated where the stubbornness was coming from. She had been forced to deal with all sorts of people during her life and was much more streetwise than him. He was convinced the recording should have gone to the police, sure it was enough to get Janos charged and locked up.

Someone has to get Janos Farkas off the streets and behind bars. The man is getting away scot free. He knew he could not defy her and go to the police. If she didn't want them involved, she simply wouldn't back him up.

He was not pleased that, yet again, he had something else to keep from Beth. This was not the way he wanted his marriage to be. He wasn't prepared to lie, but he knew it was best to keep this latest Janos outrage quiet. She was already worried Janos wanted revenge on Alison. This could only make her more anxious.

Josie opened the door. It was Gemma again, bringing more flowers.

"Is Beth in? I really want to talk to her."

Josie widened the door to let her through. "I'm busy in the kitchen and I've got the washing to put out. I'll leave you in peace." Gemma went into the little sitting room to speak to Beth while Josie returned to the kitchen and closed the door behind her.

"She really doesn't like me, does she?"

"She's very loyal to Matthew, that's all."

"Someone has to be, I suppose."

Beth ignored the inference, hiding her annoyance by putting Gwynnie on the soft baby rug on the floor and placing toys within her reach. "Nothing's wrong, is it?"

"Far from it." Gemma sat herself awkwardly on the rocking chair. Her short skirt meant achieving a state of decorum was challenging. "I was out of order with you the other day and I've come to apologise. You've always been good to me, and I know you don't get involved with Matthew's work."

"I don't," Beth said, "but I support his judgment one hundred percent."

"I know." She changed the subject. "Janos is taking me to London for the weekend. We've never been away together before. I'm so excited. I just had to tell someone."

"That's nice," Beth could think of nothing else to say.

"We're staying at Bentley's. It's got five stars and counting. He's booked us a suite."

"Is it a special occasion?"

"I hope it turns out to be. We're so close now. He's got a deal to clinch whilst we're there, but, apart from that, the time is ours. I know he wants me at the meeting, more client schmoozing, but it shouldn't take long. He's already bought me a gorgeous dress. He wants me to look the part. We went to Harvey Nicks in Leeds."

Beth looked sadly at the excited girl. She was naïve, believing her prince was on the brink of proposing to her.

"Don't look so glum," Gemma said. "It's going to be wonderful." She showed Beth pictures of their hotel on her phone.

"I hope we have time to go to the theatre. I'll want to show off my dress as much as I can whilst we're there."

"That sounds nice." Beth hated having to rely on *nice*. It was so far from her actual thoughts.

There was a pause.

"I'm on the pill now. I went to the clinic a couple of weeks ago. I took your advice about condoms, but we've been together for ages, and we're exclusive, so it's the right time. Of course, my parents don't know."

Beth was disconcerted — a couple of weeks was not her idea of ages. She couldn't understand why Gemma constantly needed to confide in her. She was disappointed, too. She hated the idea Gemma was going to put herself at risk. She was sad Diana had not been able to convince her either. They had shared their anxieties, both uneasy about Janos' prior liaisons, and neither was convinced he would be exclusive.

"You can't be too careful, Gemma. It really hasn't been all that long. As I told you before, he might put you at risk, and not even know it." She was treading with care.

"Oh, Beth! You don't know him. You've not even met him properly. It's not as though he's slept around, so you've no need to worry. He's actually very conservative when you hear him talk about family. Anyway, it's what we both want."

Beth felt awkward, not wanting to lecture further. She decided to change the subject, not wanting to say, in her opinion, he had probably been free with his favours. "Gwynnie's got a tooth."

"Are you going to stop feeding her?" Gemma shuddered.

"Of course I'm not going to stop, it's only a tiny little thing. Matthew's really proud of it." Once again, Beth was reminded just how naïve Gemma was. She also had no idea that the mention of Matthew would annoy Gemma so much and was startled by her response.

"As long as he's not proud of himself. He has no cause to be, turning down offers of help for that centre of his, just because Janos isn't grand enough. He's still furious and vowing to get his own back on that dreadful woman. You'd better warn her."

"The board turned Janos down," Beth said, "not Matthew or Alison."

"Technically, yes, but Matthew could have spoken up for him. And did you know that dreadful woman assaulted him when he went to offer help directly? That was before he knew he'd been turned down. He could have made such great connections by working with the sponsors. He could have schmoozed some influential people at the launch party. They'd have been putty in his hands. He was banking on expanding his address book at the big event."

"Gemma, Matthew definitely won't be wasting the charity's money on parties, and you know I have nothing to do with the centre. You're wasting your breath on me. I can't influence things. I accepted your apology. Let's leave it there."

"At least Janos listens to me."

Beth heard the petulance and the implication and ignored both. "I'm glad," she said, without conviction. Gemma's decision to go on the pill showed she was the one who listened to him.

She didn't stay much longer. Beth could see her excitement talking about London had faded when she became irritated about Matthew and Alison. She soon became restless and anxious to leave.

Matthew arrived home soon after Gemma had left. Beth thought he looked stressed.

"Gemma's been round. She's going away to London with Janos next weekend. She was really excited."

"That bloody man again," Matthew snapped. "It's been a difficult day. Alison and I have been talking about him until we're both sick and tired. He's the last person I want to talk about here."

"Josie's cooked up a Caribbean special for dinner. That should cheer you up." She hoped to divert his thoughts.

"Her going home would cheer me up. She's been here for ages."

"Matthew! She's lonely, and she's wonderful to have around."

"I know, but it's hard for me to be spectacular, as you so publicly put it, with her on the other side of the wall." He dropped a kiss on Gwynnie's head. "I'm going for a shower."

He went upstairs in the worst mood Beth had ever seen him in. His feet thumped on each tread and the little banister shook. She was shocked at his irritability and intolerance towards Josie after all she had done for them. She was terrified the woman might have heard what he'd said.

He was down within a minute. "I'm sorry, Beth." He put his arms around her." I didn't mean a word I said. You know Josie's welcome." He kissed her hair.

"I just hope she didn't hear you. She's only in the kitchen." She nodded at the closed door. "I'm really happy she's staying longer."

"So am I. She didn't deserve that, after all she's done for us."

Something was bothering Matthew. Janos' name had been the trigger. Beth hoped he wasn't causing trouble again.

CHAPTER SIX

Gemma could see Janos was like an excited child when they got to London. Despite his confidence and swagger, he was not familiar with the capital. After they dropped their bags off with the hotel's concierge, she took him to see the sights. She knew London well from innumerable family trips.

They did the Red Bus Tour, rode the London Eye, took a Thames River Trip, and finally managed a quick visit to the Tower.

They were glad to get back to the hotel. Their suite was available by then. Gemma could see Janos was trying to be cool about its opulence, but she made no such pretence. She was used to the good life but freely admitted she had never stayed anywhere so fabulous in her life.

He said it was all the better, because his new contacts were paying. He lost all semblance of nonchalance when he saw the spa bath. He turned the taps on immediately and started pulling his clothes off.

"Come on, baby," he said, motioning for her to do the same.

Gemma was soon leaning against him in the warm, deep, pulsing water.

"I'm glad I was your first," he said, nuzzling her neck. "The first is the most important."

"I'm glad too," she said. She was blissfully happy.

"And soon I will be the first to sow seeds inside you. Would you like that?"

She had been on the pill for a while. That should make it

okay, she thought. It should be long enough.

She was so much in love, so ecstatically in the moment that, without giving it further consideration, she murmured, "Yes."

Janos was cockier than ever when they went to dinner. Gemma thought it was because of the nature of the intimacy they'd just shared. She knew she looked stunning in the clinging, plunging, shimmering dress he'd chosen. She was looking at him in adoration and felt as if this was the start of something even more special between them.

They indulged themselves with the finest the menu could offer. Janos was revelling in the knowledge someone else was paying.

They had both enjoyed their first course, pan-fried scallops in a cream and garlic sauce. Gemma was enchanted by the presentation of her main course, but she soon saw he was staring miserably at his steak tartare.

"At that price, you'd think they could have cooked it," he muttered to Gemma, maintaining an undisturbed outer air.

She giggled. "I thought you chose it because your ancestors ate it."

"What?" He clearly had no idea what she meant. She explained she could imagine Hungarian warriors, Tartars, demolishing raw steak.

"You think I come from savages?" he asked.

"Of course not." She could see her well-meant remark had rattled him. She knew the perceived insult had robbed him of his enthusiasm for spending other people's money when he refused desert and coffee. She thought his abruptness seemed unnecessarily rude and was disappointed not to choose from the dessert menu.

He kept looking at his watch. "It's nearly ten. They'll be here in a minute. Let's go back to the suite."

"I'm scared of letting you down," she said as they entered

the lift. "I'm sorry I've annoyed you. I know you have to be at the top of your game. This deal means so much to you."

"You won't let me down," he said, leading the way into the corridor. "I'll make sure there's no chance of that."

As soon as they were in their suite, he opened the bottle of champagne that was waiting for them in the cooler.

"No more for me," she said. "I've already had enough."

"Just a drop to calm your nerves," he said.

She nodded. "Okay, but only a drop. I am so nervous I'm shaking. I've never been at such an important meeting."

"I could pop something in your drink to make you a little more relaxed. Would you like that?" His voice sounded casual, as if it was entirely up to her.

For the second time that evening she said *yes* willingly. Her trust in him was absolute as she watched him drop a pill in her glass. She was full of gratitude for his consideration.

"Thank you," she said as she waited for it to dissolve. She would be relieved when it kicked in and started to reduce her anxiety a little.

By the time there was a knock on the door her vision was blurred. She was aware that two men had entered the room, but she couldn't make out what they were saying. Their voices seemed to get further and further away. Her glass slipped from her hand, and she remembered no more.

When she woke up, she was on the floor. She was cold and she realised she was no longer wearing her beautiful dress. It struck her as strange. She didn't remember taking it off.

She eased herself to her feet and went unsteadily over to the bed. Janos stirred as she pulled back the duvet.

"What are you doing?"

"I'm cold. I'm getting into bed."

He threw a pillow on the floor. "You're sleeping there."

"I don't understand."

"I don't sleep with soiled goods."

He grabbed hold of the throw that lay on the bottom of the huge bed, tossing it at her with some force. "Cover yourself up. You disgust me." He sat up and spat at her.

She wiped her face with her hand, shaking violently. She grabbed the throw and pulled it round her.

"Filthy whore," he said, turning his back on her and pulling the duvet over him.

She picked up the throw and struggled to the sitting area. She curled up on the opulent sofa where, only hours ago, she had been glad to allow Janos to have unprotected sex with her. She pulled the cover over her shivering body.

Nothing made sense. Her head was throbbing. Her vision was blurred. Janos, the man she loved, had called her a whore. She needed to make sense of it all, but first she had to sleep. Sleep was dragging her down into an abyss that seemed to swallow her whole.

When she woke, she saw Janos was already dressed and was stuffing her beautiful dress into his shoulder bag. His suitcase was zipped and ready beside the door. He threw a handful of notes on the coffee table.

"Get the train home. Be out of here by eleven. The bill's paid up until then. After that, it's down to you."

"Janos, I don't understand."

"You're a tramp. You always were. A decent girl wouldn't have let me do the things I did to you. You've served your purpose, you slut."

"I thought you loved me."

"I despise you. I always did. But daddy will keep paying even though I've no more use for you. You clinched the deal for me, so you've served your purpose. Daddy won't want the video of how you did it going viral. I'll send you a copy. You can show it him with pride. You'd already asked me for unprotected sex. You'd already asked me to drug you. Then you, his golden girl, his little princess, willingly had wild, unprotected sex with two strangers."

He left, slamming the door behind him.

Gemma finally understood. Her world dissolved in front of her, just as the pill had dissolved in champagne the night before.

He deliberately drugged me! Worse than that, she now knew he had never loved her.

Gemma could barely handle the misery as she showered and dressed in casual clothes. She wanted to stay in the shower for ever, but she knew she had to be out of the room. She threw her things into the case she had packed with such excitement just two days before. She tossed her silver Jimmy Choo prom shoes into the waste bin. She knew she would never wear them again.

She asked the doorman to hail her a taxi. She clambered in and muttered, "Saint Pancras, please." She checked the time-table on her phone as her cab joined the heavy mid-morning traffic. She was in luck. Even at that speed, she would have time to buy a ticket and board the next train. She didn't want to be waiting about at the station in the state she was in. Far better to be huddled into her seat for the homeward journey.

She knew she had to decide what to do next as the train carried her home. Beth and her parents had been proven correct, but her battered pride was the least of her concerns. She was hurting mentally. Janos' betrayal was devastating, and all her dreams had been destroyed. She was hurting physically too, and she was starting to imagine why. Her suspicions terrified her.

She had no idea the depth of his betrayal until her phone beeped. The beeps interrupted her frantic thoughts. All of the messages were from him, and her heart leapt in hope. *It's all been a dreadful mistake and he's realised he truly loves me.*

He had sent three videos and a message. She pulled her

earphones from her pocket and connected them. She was hoping the videos would show him pleading with her to go back to him. She could not have been more mistaken.

The first video showed them sharing the spa bath when she agreed to have unprotected sex with him.

The second showed her agreeing that he provide something to calm her down before the meeting. She saw herself watching the pill dissolve in her champagne. There she was, thanking him and drinking it willingly.

The third was vile. It showed what the two men did to her when she was completely senseless. She forced herself to watch. She thought she was going to vomit as she realised what they had done.

She was in agony. It was bad enough seeing what she'd been through, but it was unbearable to know that Janos had not only filmed it but had been laughing and making evil suggestions to them. She had to force herself to watch it to the end. Realising she was hyperventilating, she closed her eyes and tried to restore natural breathing.

She had been crying since she woke, silent tears that ran in rivers down her face. She had been wiping her sleeve across her eyes and under her nose. As the video ended, the combination of her simultaneously crying and hyperventilating resulted in strange sobbing sounds escaping, but she couldn't stop it.

It didn't enter her head that she was becoming a spectacle as she absorbed the horror and started to understand why she was hurting so much. The other passengers averted their eyes and acted as if they could not see or hear her. Her desolation was complete.

She opened his final message. *If Daddy doesn't keep paying, the videos go live. Say nothing. Tell no one.*

Eventually her breathing slowed down and she forced herself to think.

She could see two possibilities. She could go home to her parents, or she could turn once more to Beth. Her instincts were telling her Beth would know what to do. She had been the one to voice practical advice ever since she entered her relationship with Janos. In her heart she knew the real reason was she couldn't face her parents. She couldn't imagine herself ever telling them what had happened.

She called Beth's number. Choosing to contact her took every ounce of her courage. "I'm on the train on my way home. Can I get a taxi and come round? Can we talk? Just us?" Her words were disjointed as her voice broke in despair.

"Whatever's wrong? What's happened?"

"I'll tell you when I see you. Can I come?"

"Of course. I'll make sure we can be alone."

Beth listened in horror as, between sobs, Gemma told her story. It was as hard for her to hear as it was for Gemma to tell. It was awakening memories she'd had to learn to keep at bay.

"We need to get your mum over here, and afterwards, you need to go to the police," Beth said. "You have to report this."

"I can't," Gemma said. She unlocked her phone and readied it for Beth to see the videos. "He's too clever. He filmed it all. I look like a willing participant, and he didn't even have to edit it."

"I can't watch," Beth said, shaking her head. She shuddered violently, fighting the panic that was rising.

"He's so clever. He managed to get me to ask for drugs and filmed me when I took them. It makes it look like I wanted all this."

"I'll phone your mum. We can't keep this from her."

"It's too humiliating," Gemma said. "She can't know."

"If you're going to get you over this, you'll need your mum," Beth said. "I'm calling her. I can't keep this from her."

Beth went into the kitchen to make her call. She knew that this would plunge Gemma into deeper despair, but it had to be done. She decided to keep it simple and leave full explanations until they were face to face.

"Gemma's here," she said. "She's a bit upset. Can you come round?"

"I thought she was in London," Diana Hooper said.

"She was, but it went badly wrong. She needs you."

"I'll come straight over."

When she went back into the living room Gemma's face was grey. She looked on the edge of collapse.

"Whatever's the matter?" she asked.

"I've shared the videos on Twitter and Facebook. I've just texted him to tell him, and to say he won't be able to blackmail my dad or me ever again."

Beth was stunned. She took her phone and went into each platform in turn. The videos were already uploaded. She needed to get the posts taken down as soon as possible for Gemma's sake. The fact they had been made public protected the Hoopers from further exploitation by Janos, but they exposed Gemma to untold repercussions. The fewer people to see them, the better.

She reported each one. When the automatic response asked for a reason, she typed, *Sexual abuse.*

She spoke as she was doing this. "That was brave," she said, "but they have to come down at once. You've been through enough. You don't need the whole world watching it too."

"At this minute, Beth, I don't care. As long as he can't use them to control me or my family," she said.

"You've certainly put a stop to him doing that," she said, "but we have to minimise the damage to you."

"I can't believe you're not furious with me," Gemma said. "You gave me enough warnings."

"You don't need my lectures. You're seeing everything all

too clearly now, and I know it hurts. I know how much you loved him."

"How did you get to be so wise?"

"I learnt the hard way," Beth said, remembering her own days of suffering. She prayed Gemma would handle the trauma better than she had. "And I'm afraid you have to face the same things I did. You and your parents will have to decide if you're going to the police. Regardless of that, you need testing for STIs. If you go to the police they'll see to it, if not, you'll have to get it done. I think you'll need the morning after pill too."

Gemma looked at Beth in despair. "Do I have to do tests?"

"You know you do," she said. "You're probably more at risk from those two men than you were from him. I'll make sure your mum knows what to do."

"Can't you come with me and sort it out? Do we have to involve her?"

Beth shook her head. "I'm sorry Gemma. It will have to be your mum." Memories of what she had been through after her rape were pushing to enter her brain. It was all too much, but she couldn't explain all that to the traumatised girl. Gemma didn't need to know.

She knew Gemma would need her mother, and she also knew Diana Hooper would never forgive her if she shut her out of this. Above all, she couldn't allow those awful memories to take her over again. She had to think of Gwynnie.

Gemma's voice jolted her back into focus. "I didn't realise just how evil he could be. I thought he loved me, and look what he's done to me. He said he always despised me."

"That's wicked," Beth agreed.

"But if he can do this to me, after all we shared, what could he do to that Armstrong woman? He never stops talking about her and what she did to him. He's obsessed."

"Don't worry about that now. You've got enough on your mind. Alison has security staff, and Matthew can warn her to take extra care. Concentrate on you."

"That won't be hard," Gemma said. "It's like my world's fallen in."

Beth realised Diana was totally unprepared for the nightmare that Gemma would share. There was nothing she could do to make it any easier, and she watched in despair as the girl told her mother everything that had happened.

Diana took her daughter in her arms and held her tight. They were both sobbing. Beth understood Diana needed time alone with her daughter. She put the lead on Sasha and said she'd go out for a while, giving them time to talk.

Her head was pounding. She didn't mind helping Diana and Gemma, she just needed to handle the impact all this had on her without them knowing. The best person to help her was Matthew. She called him as she walked, and just as she knew he would, he said he'd come at once. He was coming for her, but she also knew he'd be better equipped to support Gemma and Diana than she was.

She checked social media. The action by the platforms had been prompt. The videos had been taken down and she could see no posts about them. She felt relief as her frantic scrolling revealed nothing. She had managed to eliminate the damage to Gemma.

She had no idea where she was heading. She simply walked, head down. That day was not the day to exchange pleasantries; she ignored anyone who greeted her. Her heart was pounding. She was doing her best to handle the nausea that had overwhelmed her. Although she hadn't watched the videos, she had seen how traumatised Gemma was, and she knew her own traumas were pushing to resurface. She walked on, trying to control her breathing.

She glanced at her watch. Matthew would be home soon, and Gemma and Diana should have had time to talk. She headed back, wanting to support the Hoopers but dreading facing them again.

Gemma was curled up in her mother's arms when she returned.

Diana looked stricken. "Thanks, Beth, for everything," she said. "We've had a long talk. Gemma won't hear of going to the police. All she wants to do is go home and shower."

"I can understand that, but please think carefully. If there's any chance of going to the police, she mustn't shower again." Beth said. "Whatever you decide, she must get herself tested." She turned directly to Diana. "I'm sorry to be blunt, but she's at risk, and the sooner all the tests are done, the better."

Diana nodded. "We'll go today," she said.

"Have you been in touch with Edward?" Beth asked.

Diana shook her head. "I don't know how we're going to tell him. This is going to break him. I never understood why he'd put some business that dreadful man's way. Now I know why."

Gemma's body shook. "I'm so sorry," she said, her voice spluttering between the sobs. "He won't need to keep paying now I've posted the videos. I had no idea Janos was blackmailing him."

"Neither did I. I suppose he started that fire, too." She hugged her even more tightly, gently kissing the top of her head. "You've nothing to be sorry for. You just fell in love with the wrong man." She turned to Beth. "I forced myself to watch the videos, I'm so glad you couldn't bring yourself to. They're vile. My God, Beth, she's been used and abused. They're nothing but animals, and that bastard enjoyed every moment. She may not be going to the police, but she's going to see a doctor."

"They should be all be arrested," Beth said.

"No police. He made sure I consented to it all. I look like a prostitute in those videos." Gemma's voice sounded hysterical.

"Just keep thinking he might do it to someone else and

remember Matthew and I are here for you all," Beth said, knowing the pain that would heap on her, but saying it just the same.

"How many more times do I have to tell you?" Gemma sobbed. "No police."

"Here's Matthew now," Diana said, putting her arms round her sobbing daughter.

Matthew had come straight over, aware of some of what happened from Beth's call.

"What can I do?" he asked.

Diana let go of Gemma. "Nothing at the minute," she said. "I'm going to take Gemma home, and when she's ready, we'll head to the clinic." She stood and then extended her hand to her daughter. "Come on, angel. We'll go home now."

Gemma took it and rose slowly to her feet, wincing with discomfort.

"What about Edward?" Matthew asked.

"I'll talk to him when he comes home," Diana said. "I'll get Gemma sorted first. I'll ring you later. Perhaps you could come round, I have a feeling he'll need you."

"Whatever I can do," Matthew said. "But please go to the police."

Diana shrugged her shoulders helplessly and led Gemma out to her car.

Matthew and Beth followed.

"Thank you," Diana said. She helped Gemma into the passenger seat and leant over to fasten the belt. It was clear the girl was barely functioning, and it reminded Beth of the catatonic state she had known so well.

When the Hoopers had driven away and they were back in the cottage, she collapsed into Matthew's arms. As always, she didn't need to explain how she felt. They were soulmates. He understood. He hugged her close and they stayed locked in each other's arms until Beth's sobs subsided.

Matthew went round to the Hoopers' house as soon as Diana called. He took Edward to the village pub. He knew he'd need to talk freely, and it was obvious they couldn't do that with Diana and Gemma in the house.

Matthew could see he was devastated. His face was ashen, and his eyes looked sore. Above all else, he was angry. He said he was angrier than he ever knew he could be, and he kept clenching his fists.

"Bloody secrets," he said. "This is all my fault. I kept quiet about that bastard blackmailing me to protect Diana and Gemma. Look where that got Gemma. If I'd been straight with them, and more of a father, maybe Gemma would have walked away from him there and then."

Matthew knew it was a time to listen. Edward was trying to come to terms with what Janos had put Gemma through. Saying the same things over and over was helping him process the nightmare that had unfolded.

Eventually, he started to get his thoughts in order. "Gem won't hear of going to the police because of those videos. Diana agrees they make her look like a willing participant, so that's another thing he's gotten away with."

"You've not watched them?"

'No, and I'm not going to. That first one still makes me want to vomit, and I never watched that to the end."

Matthew sensed he could address the essentials now. "Has Gemma been to the clinic?"

"Diana took care of all that, thank God. Now we've got to wait, maybe up to ten days, to know if she's okay. Poor kid, she's done nothing but take showers since they got back. She can barely look Diana and I in the face, she's so ashamed."

Matthew nodded. "I can see how hard it is for you and Diana, but Gemma's world fell in yesterday and today she has had to face all the people who warned her she was making a mistake. Worst of all, she's got to face up to how naïve she was. It's going to take her a long time."

Edward looked at him as if he was shocked. "I'd not looked at it like that. What sort of father am I? All I've thought about is how I want to get my hands on that animal and what I'd do to him. Gemma must be going through absolute hell. I've hugged her, of course, and told her everything will be okay, but I wasn't really thinking about what she's going through."

"At the moment, she won't be blaming you for that. She knows what they did to her, and she knows he stood back and filmed it. She'll be battered and bruised, and she'll be feeling stupid and guilty and betrayed all at the same time. She's going to need you for a long time."

"As long as it takes," he said, taking a long drink from his pint. "You sound as if you know what you're talking about. Your line of work, I suppose, listening to people's tales of woe."

Matthew knew this was not the time to share. "Something like that," he said. "Did you ever tell Diana that Janos started the fire at the shop?"

Edward shook his head. "She knows now. I've had to tell her about the video he was holding. I should have told her from the start. I've told them both now, but it's too late. Diana's seen videos far worse than that one, God help her. She's taking care of Gemma right now, but I'll need to be there to take care of her when she finally buckles. I think she'll be okay whilst she's fussing around. It will hit her when things calm down."

"Just like she'll be there for you," Matthew added. "And, of course, Beth and I are there for you all."

Edward sighed. "You're a funny man of God. You never seem shocked by anything, and yet you seem so . . .innocent. And you never push the church down our throats, not even when we're facing something like this."

"The church will be there for you when you want it to be," he said. "Right now, I just want to do all I can to help you all through this mess."

From then on, Edward talked and talked in circles once again. Matthew listened until Edward looked up at the clock. He was shocked by how late it was. "Can you run me back home? It's time I was there for Diana. I think I've calmed down enough now to be of some use."

"Sounds good to me."

They drove to the Hoopers' house in silence. Edward had talked himself out and Matthew was brooding over memories that had resurfaced in him that day.

Matthew knew Beth had been brave when she insisted he should go to see Edward Hooper. He could only imagine what memories that day had awoken in her and he'd hated leaving her to face them alone. He was glad to get home.

Josie and Gwynnie were in bed, fast asleep.

"Let's go to bed," he said. "I need to have you in my arms all night."

"Exactly where I need to be," she said, following him upstairs.

CHAPTER SEVEN

B eth was stunned when Gemma next visited. Six weeks had passed since the day she'd arrived on the doorstep from London, broken and betrayed.

The glamorous young woman had been erased, but the lively schoolgirl had not resurfaced. In her place was a world-weary woman. She was wearing her customary skinny jeans and trainers but had buried herself in a large, shapeless sweatshirt.

Beth remembered that desire to disappear into the folds of anonymous, androgynous clothing so well.

The long platinum hair had gone. It was chopped into an edgy style and her natural much darker blonde colour was showing. It suited her, but it gave her a waif-like vulnerability she' never had before.

Beth took her hands in hers and squeezed them gently. She saw her fingernails were raw and angry looking. Gemma had torn off her false nails.

"The new me. The fool is dead. Long live the fool," Gemma said bitterly. She looked at Gwynnie and shook her head. "This little lady is growing so fast. Let's hope she doesn't make my mistakes." She picked her up.

Gwynnie wasn't confident with this new version of Gemma and struggled to be free. She looked at Beth, holding up her arms for her mum to rescue her.

"I like your new hairstyle," Beth said.

"I chopped it off myself. It's hardly a style."

"It still suits you," she said, putting the little girl onto the floor and watching her totter across to her toys.

"She wasn't walking the last time I saw her," Gemma said.

"She took off on her own last week. She's got Josie and me running after her all day." She looked at Gemma. "How are you?"

"I came to let you know the STI tests all came back negative," she said.

"Thank God," Beth breathed heavily. "Matthew will be relieved too."

Gemma nodded. "I know you tried to warn me, Beth, but, back then, I thought I knew everything."

"You were in love," Beth said. "It blinded you to everything."

"Don't make excuses for me. I was a selfish bitch. Did you know it was Janos who set fire to my dad's shop?"

"Not at the time. I do now."

"He filmed us the first time we had sex. I thought we were making love. He was using it to blackmail my dad, and I thought he was in love with me. He can't blackmail us anymore, not since I put those videos online. He knows if I was willing to post the bad ones, I wouldn't hesitate to post the one he sent to my dad."

"It was incredibly brave of you to do that," Beth said. "I couldn't have done it."

"It was my penance. I had to get him out of our lives for good, no matter what the cost to my reputation. After the way I'd behaved, it was what I deserved. Did you know he threatened to get me hooked on heroin if Dad didn't pay up?"

"Matthew told me. Gemma, we have to be positive. That didn't happen. You've got to look forward."

Beth saw Gemma shudder and then straighten up and put a smile on her face.

"I need a fresh start," she said. "My parents have been great, but I can't go on torturing them. Me being in the same room makes them feel awkward. My mum watched the entire set of videos. My dad hasn't, but he knows what's on them. They can hardly look me in the face. I've done them enough harm. I won't keep on hurting them."

"They know you weren't to blame. They know you were the victim. I'm sure they're doing their best. They need time, Gemma, just like you do. It's been awful for you all."

"What I did with Janos was entirely my choice. I was stupid enough to believe it was love. I have to face up the aftermath of what those men did to me. I can't dump it on my parents."

Her words troubled Beth. The tests had been negative, and she knew Edward and Diana's support had never wavered. "Are you keeping something back from them?"

There was a pause and then Gemma nodded her head. "I'm leaving," she said.

"Don't just disappear, Gemma. They've been through enough. They'd search high and low to find you."

Gemma sat quietly for a few moments. "Why do you always have to be my conscience? You always remind me what I should be doing. I was just going to take off and move somewhere new. Get a fresh start. Let them forget me. I know I can find work. I can do waitressing or shop work."

"I guess it's because I know how much they love you," Beth replied. "They'd never just forget you. They wouldn't rest if you just disappeared. They'd search to the ends of the earth to find you. Talk to them. If you have to go away, make sure they know where you are, and for God's sake, keep in touch with them. You've put them through enough through no fault of your own. This would be your fault." Beth could see Gemma was thinking through what she had just said. There was a long pause and she prayed she'd got through to her.

"I'll sort it," Gemma said at last. "I just came by to thank you for standing by me. I didn't deserve your support. Now you've sorted me out again. When did you get to be so wise?"

"That's a long story," Beth said, "and it's certainly not one for today."

"Thank Matthew for me too, please. Most of all, please look out for my mum and dad when I've gone."

"We both will, but you must talk to them. Don't just take off."

"I promise I'll talk to them," Gemma said. She stood up and moved over to drop a kiss on Gwynnie's head. "Thanks, Beth. For everything. I'll see myself out."

She left and Beth was in a panic. She wasn't sure Gemma would keep her word. She was scared she'd just take off. She had seen how much the girl was still hurting and struggling with her shame. She hadn't made any promises to Gemma, other than to look out for her parents so her decision came easily. Looking out for them meant keeping them informed.

She popped more toys on the floor to entertain Gwynnie and picked up her phone. She knew she had to call Diana Hooper.

Beth was relieved when Diana called in later to say Gemma kept her word. She had gone straight home and told her mother her plans.

"Nothing would deter her," she said.

Beth could see she had been crying.

"I begged her to stay but she's tormented with guilt. She says she can't keep facing me and her dad with all that on her conscience. It's tragic. We love her, we've not offered a word of reproach, but she still can't be in the same room as us. She feels she has let us down."

"I'm sorry, Diana. I did my best to get her to stay," Beth replied.

"I know. If it wasn't for you, we both think she'd have just taken off. As it is, she's promised to text every week. God knows how she'll cope. She wouldn't say where she was going. At least we were seeing her when she was with that animal. Now we don't know when we'll see her again. I could kill him, Beth, I really could."

"I'm sure Edward feels the same. At least you're all out of his clutches now."

Diana nodded. "Edward kept a lot from me. I thought he was just putting a bit of business his way to build bridges. I had no idea he was being blackmailed. At least Gemma put paid to that, Edward's stopped paying and he's not heard a word since. I don't know how she got the courage to release those videos."

"It was brave. Hopefully not many people saw them."

"We've got you to thank for getting them taken down. What happened to my girl will stay with me forever, and I feel as if it's all my fault. I can't get those videos out of my head. I should have stopped her seeing him."

"None of us could have done that. She really loved him," Beth said. "His betrayal was the most wicked thing I've heard of."

"You might be right, but I still feel responsible, and I know Edward does too. He's demented at the thought of her leaving home. He's got some idea of tracking her down."

"She'll come home, but not until she's ready. She has a lot to process," Beth said.

Later that day, Beth needed to get out of the house, so she offered to drive Josie over to her home. Josie had mentioned several times that she needed to check the property and pick up the mail.

"There's no need to go rushing over there today," Josie said. "I can see that girl's upset you again. We could stay in and have a cup of tea and a chat."

"I have to get out of the house for a while, Josie. Anyway, you said you need to check everything's okay."

"Yes, but it doesn't have to be now."

Beth detected reluctance in her voice but pushed ahead with her plan, thinking her friend didn't want to put her to any trouble.

Josie was quiet on the drive over. Eventually Beth pulled the temperamental old Fiesta in front of a neat semi-detached house. The front garden was paved for car parking, so there was no sign of weeds or neglect. Beth turned off the engine and turned to Josie. She was astonished to see she was shaking.

"Whatever's wrong?"

"I can't go in," Josie said. She pulled out a tissue and wiped the tears away.

Beth had never seen Josie like that. She was always upbeat and capable, able to face anything. She turned and checked on Gwynnie. She had dozed during the drive and was now fast asleep.

"Beth, take me home."

"Shall I just pop in to check everything and collect your mail, beings as we're here?" Beth offered. "You can stay here with Gwynnie."

Josie made a snuffling sound. "No. You can't go in. I'll make myself do it, but not today. I know Matthew has had enough of me staying with you, I heard him say so, so I'll do it soon."

Beth recalled the evening when Matthew had been exasperated with Janos, and he had let off some steam. The subject of Josie had got caught up in his outburst and he had later admitted that he hadn't meant what he said. It was the night Josie had made them a special Caribbean meal and she had been in the kitchen when Matthew had exploded. She had obviously heard every word.

She took Josie's hand. There was no point denying what he had said, but she could make Josie understand that none of his frustration had been about her. She tried her best to explain. She said all she knew was he'd been furious when she mentioned Janos and had let off some steam.

Josie dabbed her eyes. "I can't stay with you forever, but I can't come back here. After Sidney died, all that was left was the silence. Before I came to stay with you, I used to take the bus into town every day and walk round the shops until teatime. If you go in, you'll see what I'm so ashamed of. When I go in, I'll have to face it again, and I don't want to."

Beth was starting to feel alarmed. What was it that Josie didn't want her to see? What was Josie afraid to face? She had visions of an Aladdin's cave of stolen goods from shop lifting sprees and was already trying to think what they would do with it all. If no one had gone to the police about Janos, she certainly wouldn't be going about Josie. She could see the headlines. *Vicar's wife dumps stolen goods.*

She pulled herself together. "Josie, after all we've been through, we can face anything together," she said, not believing a word she uttered. She had visions of herself fly-tipping stolen goods in the dead of night. She wasn't sure what alarmed her the most, the fly-tipping or the stolen goods.

"You've been through too much. I can't land my problems on you as well," Josie said. Her voice was breaking with sobs. "I'm so ashamed."

"Give me your keys," Beth said, her heart beating fast. "I'll go in, pick up your mail and then we'll go back home. We'll have a cup of tea, and you can tell me all about it."

Josie took out a bunch of keys, separated the front door key and handed it over. Beth went to the front door in a state of dread, feeling as if she was about to become an accomplice. The wooden front door had swollen with the damp, and she had to exert some force to open it. She was surprised by the resistance she could feel behind the door once it was unfastened. She had to squeeze through a tiny gap.

She was confronted by mountains of newspapers. It looked as if Josie hadn't picked any up since Sidney's funeral. She'd not bothered to cancel delivery, even when she'd gone to stay with them. Beth could see that day's headlines on the topmost paper.

There was a huge mound of morning papers, evening papers, magazines, local free sheets, advertising bumph and mail to get across. They moved as she trod on them, slithering against each other, making her struggle to keep her footing.

Josie had been houseproud. Beth remembered how immaculate the house had been the day of Sidney's funeral. As she peeped into the rooms, she realised Josie had simply stopped caring. Every room was the same. Not only were they thick with dust and stale from lack of use, they were cluttered with debris and dirty plates and dishes. The kitchen was the worst. It looked as if Josie had started leaving dishes in the other rooms when the kitchen could take no more. She must have worked her way through every pot and pan she owned and never washed one of them. It was chaotic, and the little room stank of rotting food and dirty drains.

Every milk carton, tin or wrapping was spilling over the waste bin and covering the floor. The stench was overwhelming. Unable to stand it anymore, she shut the door and headed back to the front door.

She sifted through the mountain of newspapers to pull together what letters she could find and struggled out to secure the door. Shame swept over her. She'd imagined Josie had turned into a shoplifter when the woman had actually plunged into a spiral of despair and had been hiding it from everyone.

She got back into the car and put her arms round Josie. "Why didn't you say?" she asked. "Matthew and I love you so much. You could have told us how bad things were. We'd have been there for you."

"Can I stay with you a bit longer?" Josie asked, snuffling.

"Of course you can. You can stay for as long as you like. Anyway, there's no way you can think of going back there until we sort it out."

Josie returned her hug. "I never wanted anyone to see it. I never wanted to set foot in there again."

Beth remembered Matthew saying Josie had been standing out on the pavement waiting for him, the night he fetched her over to stay. Now she could understand why. "I'll help you when you're ready. There's no rush."

"Will you have to tell Matthew?"

"Would you have told Sidney?" Beth asked, knowing Josie had told him everything.

She was troubled as they headed home. She didn't know how they would cope in the long term. Gwynnie would soon be needing a bed, and though her little room would just about take that, there would be no room for Josie's.

She was ashamed she had never sensed how much Josie had struggled after Sidney's funeral. Josie had never let it show, and she had failed her friend miserably.

She couldn't talk things over with Matthew until they were in bed. Curled up together in the dark, he listened as Beth told him about the day's events.

He was full of praise when he heard that she'd managed to get Gemma to tell her parents she was leaving home. He loved his wife beyond words and was always amazed at how wise and kind she was to everyone.

He was troubled by her revelations about the state of Josie's home and the misery she felt there. "She can stay as long as she likes, but we really will have to find a bigger place," he said. "The trouble is, I don't think we can afford to pay much more rent."

Beth nodded. "I hate to say it, but turning down a pay rise hasn't helped. We need a bigger place regardless of Josie. We can just about squeeze a bed into her room, but there's no space for anything else. We'll have to move then." she said. "If Josie stays on, maybe I could build up the accounting business again. She'd be able to take care of Gwynnie while I work. Perhaps she could pay a little bit herself if she lets her house go. There were a lot of bills amongst the mail I picked up. I hope she's not got into a mess."

"I doubt it. She's not used any gas or electricity whilst she's been here, and she's not been out spending money. I'm sure she'll be fine. To be honest, if your business does pick up again, we should be able to look for somewhere bigger. We can manage for a bit longer here."

"That makes sense, but please don't turn down any more pay rises," Beth said. "By the way, she did hear you that night when you talked about her leaving. You'll have to apologise. I told her she could stay with us because I can't see her ever going back, even if we clean it up. When we got there, she just couldn't go in."

"Poor woman," he said. "I'll explain I was just letting off steam that day. She hides her feelings well. I had no idea she wasn't coping and had let things go. I suppose I'd be exactly the same without you." He pulled her close.

She snuggled against him, breathing in the scent of his skin.

'Right now, I'm so grateful to have you, all I want to do is make love to you," he said. His voice was soft and caring. "Quietly and gently, just like when we stayed together at the Willows and the Grace children were in the next room."

"We were lovers then," she said.

"And always will be."

The centre was ready to open. The decorations and furnishing were complete, and the staff had been trained. Volunteers had come forward. Everyone had been police checked and had undertaken training. Matthew was relieved to know that there was adequate staffing to cope with the expected number of clients. He remembered all too clearly how over-stretched he had been.

Alison argued for a big opening event, but Matthew persuaded her that ostentation went against the ethos of the place. Just as Beth had expected, he wanted a low-key affair. He was more interested in making sure the people who needed it knew it existed, so he'd invested in signage.

Alison said she could see the sense in what he said but insisted she would organise a fund-raiser to lift the charity's profile. She explained that the event would be entirely self-financing, and they could use it to launch the fundraising for the next centre. Derby had been earmarked for the expansion.

Matthew begged her to invest her energy into the new project, but she insisted that was exactly what she would be doing. She seemed convinced the event would raise enough to give them a flying start in Derby.

As soon as the board gave their approval, she threw herself into organising a ticketed, black-tie dinner at Brooksley Hall. She told Matthew she knew the owner well and said he had been forced into the events business to raise funds for the hall's upkeep. She knew he'd be glad of the business and publicity it would generate and would offer a good deal.

Alison insisted it needed to be on the grand scale. She had learned the business benefits of such charity events in the past. She reassured Matthew she would rein in her flamboyant taste in favour of refinement and elegance. He was relieved not to have to fight that battle.

He was staggered by the guest list. He had expected to see their sponsors there, but Alison had invited all the grandees from miles around. He could see the charity would benefit in the long term, so he went along with her plans, wincing inwardly at the extravagance. He muttered he was sure he could have put the money to better use.

"I've told you it will be self-funding and will raise a load of money. I don't know how Beth puts up with your stingy ways," she grumbled. "I hope you'll let her have a new dress for the big night."

"Beth and Josie are re-working the living room curtains as

we speak," he said, grinning.

Alison looked at him blankly.

"Scarlet O'Hara. Gone With the Wind."

She gave him a friendly shove. "I'm serious, Matthew. It's okay for you. You'll just put on your tux and away you'll go. Sorted. Even if Beth forgot to iron your dress shirt, you could put your dog collar on and get away with it. It's not so easy for her."

"Beth looks beautiful no matter what she wears," he replied.

"That's very noble of you," Alison replied, "but it misses the point completely."

"You'll see," he said with a confidence he no longer had. He had realised Beth would have nothing to wear and they couldn't afford a fancy outfit for her. He knew now why she had insisted she wouldn't be going. She'd said it was his night and she didn't want to be in the way. He had forced the issue, saying he needed her, and she had eventually agreed. Now he finally understood her reluctance.

"Alison's in full flow getting this gala dinner sorted," he said when he returned home. "She made me realise you don't have anything to wear. I'm so sorry. I didn't mean to cause you problems."

"You haven't," she said. "Diana Hooper's going to pass something on. She says there's a few dresses to choose from that she's fed up with, and she doesn't mind me having to make alterations. Josie's going to see to that."

Matthew felt a wave of relief wash over him. He was also reminded how quietly supportive his wife always was.

"Have the Hoopers decided if they're going?"

"Diana says they are. They want to support you, even though they don't feel like partying."

Matthew nodded appreciatively. "Is Gemma keeping in touch with them?"

"She texts once a week. Diana says she hasn't said where she is, but she's told them she's found a job as a receptionist at a hotel, and she's got a room in the staff quarters."

"Could be worse," he said.

"I just hope she's telling the truth."

"So do I. At least she's kept her word about staying in contact. You haven't heard from her, have you?"

Beth shook her head. "That should mean everything's as okay as it can be. She's always come to me when she's needed help." She changed the subject. "I've asked Marie to let her friends know I'm back in business. She's sure they'll come back to me." Marie ran the deli-café in their old village, and Beth had done her bookkeeping for some time.

"That's reassuring," he said. "They were always happy with your work."

"They liked my rates," she replied, realistic as always. "I'm cheap."

"It's sad we need to move. We've been happy here," he said, looking round the little room, "but we can be happy anywhere, as long as the three of us are together."

"True."

There was only one of Diana's unwanted dresses that Josie could adapt for Beth's tiny frame. It was designed to cling to the body and was in a shimmering cream material with a black collar detail.

"I can't wear a dress like that," she said as she held it up. "It's slinky, and it's positively indecent at the back. What would everyone think?"

"Try it on before you reject it," Josie said. "It's quite modest at the front."

Beth slipped the dress on reluctantly.

"Look in the mirror, girl," Josie said. "They'll think Matthew's a very lucky man."

Beth peeped cautiously in the mirror. The front view was reassuringly demure, so she twisted to take in the back view. Her reflection astonished her. It showed a slender, sophisticated woman.

She couldn't believe how amazing she felt when she was swathed in its sensuous folds.

"I'm not sure I'd dare wear it," she said.

"You're a fool if you don't," Josie said. "You look like a duchess."

"I'll think about it," she said. "I've always got my tea dress."

"Tea dress! That old thing! You're not going to a gala in that," Josie said.

"I'll think about it," Beth said again.

She thought about little else and tried the dress on several times before deciding to wear it. She managed to find a pair of unworn cream shoes encrusted with pearls in the local charity shop. They had low but flattering heels, so she knew she wouldn't embarrass herself by stumbling off them. She got them for five pounds, but she knew the previous owner, whoever she was, would have spent a fortune on them.

"It's a pity they didn't get worn," she said. "I expect there's a sad story here."

Josie had laughed at her sentimentality. "Just be pleased you've got them," she said. "Some things are meant to be. Just wait till Matthew sees you all dolled up."

Beth was shaking with apprehension as she came downstairs on the night of the gala. She was embarrassed to admit to herself she felt glamorous.

She had kept the dress and shoes hidden from Matthew, and had insisted on him leaving her alone to get ready.

He was waiting for her in the living room.

"Beth!" he said.

"I'll go and change," she said immediately.

"You'll do no such thing. I've never seen you look more beautiful," he said. "I can't wait to show you off."

"I told you he'd approve," Josie said. "Now go and enjoy yourselves."

They took a taxi to the gala. Alison had forbidden either of them coming to help set the event up, ensuring the whole thing would come as a surprise. The hall was themed in silver and white from the reception room, through to the dining room, through to the ballroom. There were waiters everywhere holding silver trays laden with drinks and canapes.

"Good grief," Beth whispered to Matthew. "How much has this lot cost?"

"A fortune," he said. "Alison sold tables to wealthy individuals and businesses. Only our current sponsors are here as non-paying guests. Lord knows what the ticket price was."

"We wouldn't have been able to afford tickets to your own gala dinner," Beth giggled. She was suddenly more serious. "Stay with me until the Hoopers get here. I don't know anyone."

"When you look as wonderful as you do this evening, I will be glued to your side."

She squeezed his arm and sipped her champagne, taking in the magnificence of the floral decorations and breathing in the heady scent of white lilies.

Alison had done an amazing job. She came over at just that moment, a vision in fuchsia pink chiffon and ostrich feathers. Only Alison could get away with a look like that, Beth thought. The woman was magnificent that evening, and she knew it.

"Alison," Beth said, "this is wonderful. You look wonderful."

"And you look absolutely ravishing. But it's what your husband and I are trying to do at the centre that matters tonight. I'm just hoping this evening kicks off the funds for our next venture." She lowered her voice to a whisper. "I haven't told Matthew, but there's going to be a charity auction. It should raise thousands."

"You're full of surprises," Beth whispered back.

"Too damned right," Alison laughed. "Must go. People to see. Wallets to squeeze."

The food was sensational, the wines were excellent, the speeches were brief. The charity auction was even more successful than Alison had dared to imagine. Beth was trying to keep a running total in her head but gave up at twelve thousand pounds.

She turned to Matthew, watching his astonishment as the bids spiralled, enjoying his delight. "You deserve this," she said. She raised her glass to him. "A flying start for the Derby centre."

He shook his head. "Some of these people are paying silly money for a helicopter ride or a spa treatment, yet they wouldn't hand over a penny when I approached them. Double standards."

"Relax," she said. "They're supporting you now. That's what matters."

"I suppose."

Beth had never danced with Matthew before. She hadn't known he could dance. It was a good job he could, as her ballroom skills were limited. He knew how to lead, and she thought with a smile, she was always happy to follow where he was concerned.

That night, apart from the waltz Alison demanded of him, they hardly sat down. There was something intimate about being in his arms that night. The lighting was soft, and the music was perfect. The only interruptions to Beth's reverie occurred when people slapped Matthew on the back to congratulate him, interrupting the rhythm of their dancing.

It was getting towards midnight when the mood changed from sophisticated soirée to party time, so they decided to make their excuses whilst the magic of their night was intact.

They found Alison deep in conversation with someone she introduced as Lord Brooksley. Both instantly realised he was the venue's owner.

"I've heard a lot about you," he said to Matthew. "This lady rates you very highly."

Matthew nodded in acknowledgment. "That's praise indeed, coming from such a power force as Alison."

The man slipped his arm round Alison's waist. "She's wonderful, isn't she?"

Alison never ceased to amaze Beth. She instantly suspected Alison had snared herself a lord of the realm.

"Brooksie has a property in Derby that's going to come available in a couple of months. I've persuaded him it would be ideal for our next venture."

"That's amazing. Thank you both. I'm so glad you're staying on board, Alison. It's marvellous for Matthew," Beth said.

Alison nodded. "We've got our start-up funding from tonight's shindig," she said. "Onwards and upwards. If the board agree, we can get going."

"I can't see them saying no. You've put us on the map tonight in a way we never dreamed of," Matthew said.

"That's my girl," Lord Brooksley said.

Beth noted the adoring look he gave Alison.

"Never still. Always looking for the next challenge."

"Let's get your coats," Alison said to Beth. "We'll leave these two to get acquainted. They can meet us at the door."

She led Beth towards the cloakroom.

"We didn't bring coats," Beth protested.

"I know. I just wanted to let Brooksie and Matthew have a couple of minutes together. Matthew will soon see it's a perfect fit. Brooksie will come on board if he does."

"You sound very certain," Beth said.

"Sweetie, he wants to marry me. He'll come on board, trust me." She said it as if it was the most natural thing in the world for him to do as she said.

"Oh, my goodness." Beth was stunned. "What did you say?"

"I said I'm not sure I want to make him husband number four," she said. "I'll be rivalling Liz Taylor at the rate I'm going." She laughed.

"Alison, you're terrible," Beth said.

"Not really. I'm very fond of him, and he treats me as if I'm a lady, which is nice, considering how common I am. And he's wonderful in bed."

"I was right," Beth said. "You are terrible, but you're pretty amazing too."

Beth told Matthew of their conversation as the taxi took them home.

"I've never known anyone like her. She deserves a title in her own right. She's a titan in the food industry, and now she's becoming a genuine champion of the underprivileged."

She nodded. She could think of several businesswomen who'd been ennobled for their contributions to industry and their philanthropy. "What did you think of Lord Brooksley?"

"I'm not sure," Matthew said. "I don't know if he's stepping forward to impress Alison, or if he's genuinely wanting to help. I don't want to get involved with him if he's going to back out if things sour between them."

"So wise," Beth said, "and such a good dancer. I'm a lucky woman."

He grinned. "You are, and I'm feeling particularly spectacular tonight."

"Crikey," she said, smiling. "I wonder what time Alison will get away tonight."

"She'll probably stay over. I'm sure his lordship would like that, and I can't see an early finish. I've got an idea the real party has only just started."

Matthew's phone rang at 5.30 a.m. He had long been used to night calls in his days as a parish priest and picked it up after just one ring. He had taken the call before Beth had rallied from her deep sleep.

"It was Lord Brooksley," he told her after ending the call. "He's at the hospital with Alison. Someone drove her off the road this morning, and the car overturned."

Beth was alarmed. "I thought she was staying over at the hall. Is she badly hurt?"

"She's in Xray right now, then they want to do a brain scan. I'm heading over there right now." He was pulling on clothes as he spoke.

"Who would do such a thing?" Beth asked.

"A drunk driver?" he suggested, whilst thinking it could have been someone with a grudge. He did not want to share that fear with Beth.

"The scan was just a precaution. I'd bashed my head," Alison told him. She was in the accident and emergency department. She was wearing a hospital gown and had a dressing on her forehead, just above her right eye. It looked incongruous with the smeary full make up and extravagant false lashes from the night before. "Don't panic. They didn't find anything wrong. I've just a few stitches in my hairline to show for the drama, and a throbbing headache."

"And the X-rays?"

"Just a few crushed ribs," she said. "I'm very lucky. It hurts to breathe, but my lungs are fine."

He took hold of her hand and squeezed it.

"I've not spoken to the police yet," she added.

"What happened?"

"Brooksie, can you get Matthew a cup of coffee please? He looks as if he's going to pass out."

As soon as they were alone, she told Matthew what had happened. "I left at around three. Brooksie wanted me to stay over, but I just wanted my own bed. He couldn't come with me as he had to see all the hired help off the premises and lock up. I saw no sign of another car for the first few miles. It was only when I got on to the road near the house, the one that runs alongside the river, I realised there was a car behind me. It was getting lighter by then, and I saw his face in the mirror. It was him. Fucking Farkas."

Matthew's heart lurched. It was going to be just as he'd feared.

"It all happened so fast. He shunted me from behind a few times. The last shunt was the worst and I lost control of the steering. The car rolled as I went through the hedge and it came to a halt, upside down, front end hanging over the riverbank. I was so lucky, Matthew."

"My God. Did he stop?"

"He roared off."

"So, how did you get rescued?"

"Voice recognition was still working so I was able to call for help. The fire crew got there quickly but they couldn't just pull me out. They had to stabilise the car first to stop it going into the river. You could say they kept me hanging about," she said, "upside down too."

Matthew didn't laugh.

"When they'd freed me, the ambulance crew brought me here."

"And you'd not told Brooksley about our *friend*?"

She shook her head. "I have now. He knew nothing of what had been going on. He'd have waded straight in." She sighed heavily. "I'm going to tell the police. I know I said Ivan and the boys could handle him, but this has proved me wrong. I'm going to have to involve the centre as part of the story. I'm so sorry."

"That's the least of your worries. He could have killed you. He tried to murder you."

She nodded. "I wanted you to know so you can let the Hoopers know. They may want to press charges, too. He may as well go away for as long as possible. That . . . animal . . . must have heard about the gala and staked it out. He must have followed me when I left."

"You think he was there last night?"

She nodded. "He couldn't not know about our shindig. There was so much press coverage. He'd know which way I'd go home, there's only the one route. He must have held back for miles and then caught up with me. I only saw him when I got alongside the river."

Matthew closed his eyes for a second. He was thinking about the Hoopers. They had been at the gala and had shared a table with him and Beth. They were trying to get themselves together after Gemma's departure, and this would rake everything up again.

"I'm sorry, Matthew. You were right all along. I should have gone to the police."

"And so should Edward Hooper," he said. "But that's all in the past. We need to get him put inside."

"The police are waiting to talk to me. Could you stay whilst I do all that? You can back me up about the centre."

'Of course."

Brooksley returned with the coffee, handing it to Matthew.

"She's told you what that swine did?" he asked.

Matthew nodded.

"He could have killed her. I should have made her stay with me." He turned to Alison. "Thank God you're going to tell the police. If only you had stayed with me, then none of this would have happened."

"You don't know what would have happened. You could have both ended up dead," Matthew said. "There's no knowing what he would have done, so there's no point troubling yourself with regrets."

"Let's let the police in then. The sooner they catch the bastard, the better." He looked at Alison. "Are you ready for that, my darling?"

Alison straightened up in bed, wincing with the pain. "Yes," she said.

Matthew watched Brooksley go off to find the waiting officers. He wondered how much pain could have been avoided if Edward Hooper and Alison had taken his advice in the first place. He was not a man for *I told you so,* but he couldn't avoid thinking *what if.*

Matthew listened in on the police interview and was able to corroborate Alison's story of Janos' thwarted attempts to get involved with the centre.

Alison told of the recording she was holding of the time Janos had tried to threaten her into paying him protection money. She was her usual frank self, totally honest about the pain she'd inflicted on him on both occasions.

Matthew was asked to go to the station to make a statement as soon as he could. He said he'd do that after he had called on some friends to update them. He was hoping he could persuade the Hoopers to act now that Gemma was safely out of the way. They could bring their story to the police's attention, too.

Alison was going to be detained in hospital overnight, as her heart rate and blood pressure readings were both a little high, but beyond that period of observation she would be discharged.

Brooksley was staying on with her and was going to arrange for a private room. He vowed he wouldn't leave her side, so Matthew felt free to go.

He drove over to the Hoopers. They were both at home that

morning, recovering from the excesses of the gala night. Both looked tired and pale. He told them about the attempt Janos had made on Alison's life.

"I knew he was bad news," Edward said, "but I never thought he'd go that far."

"Gemma told Beth he was out for revenge. He believed getting involved with the centre was a ticket to mixing with the great and good. It must have driven him mad to hear about the gala. It's a pity I didn't realise Alison was at risk last night."

Diana broke the stunned silence. "He has to be stopped, Edward. You have to go to the police about the fire." Diana looked at Matthew for support, but he said nothing. The decisions had to be theirs.

Edward sighed. "I've spent all this time protecting Gemma. I'm not sure I want her name dragged through the mud."

"Gem put those awful videos on Twitter to put a stop to him," Diana said. "It's too late to be worried about her reputation. This is our chance. The man is an animal and enough is enough."

"Gemma knows that what he did to her wouldn't stand up in court," Edward said. "She agreed to everything he did. The videos put him in the clear."

"I'm talking about the fire and the extortion money you handed over," Diana said.

"I signed contracts," Edward said. "It all looks above board. We know he was clever to protect himself the way he did. What do you think, Matthew?"

"I think the police and the DPP should decide if they want to prosecute, based on the evidence. They can't decide if you don't give them chance."

"True. Maybe we should talk it over with Gem first."

Diana nodded. "She'd hate it if we went ahead without telling her first."

"If she'll pick up." He turned to Matthew. "She restricts us to one brief call a week now, which she always makes. She has never picked up when we call."

"I'll text her to say something awful has happened and ask her to call you immediately. I'm sure she'll respond," Matthew said.

The Hoopers looked at each other and nodded. He picked up his phone and sent the message.

Gemma called them within five minutes.

Matthew listened to Diana telling Gemma what had happened. She asked if she would support Edward if he went to the police. He heard her emphatic reply. They were to go about the extortion, but under no account were they to mention her experiences in London. Those, she said, were down to her own stupidity.

As soon as the call ended, Edward said he would go with Matthew to the station. He looked like a defeated man as he gathered his wallet, keys and phone together.

"We should be visiting Gemma at university, not trying to pursue that animal through the courts. This is all down to my weakness. The harm that man has done to this family will never be put right by a jail sentence."

"It's better than nothing," Diana said, giving him a hug. "Do you want me to come with you?"

Edward shook his head. "No, thank you. This is a mess I created all by myself."

"I'd have done exactly the same," she said. "Never doubt that. I'd have put Gem first."

CHAPTER EIGHT

Whilst Matthew was busy with Alison and the Hoopers, Beth took the opportunity to convince Josie they should make a start on cleaning her house.

"Matthew wants to look for somewhere bigger so you can stay with us permanently. We've started looking. The embarrassing thing is, Josie, we'd have to ask you to pay rent to help us afford it."

There was absolute silence for what seemed like an age and then Josie let out an enormous sob.

"I didn't mean to upset you," Beth said.

"You haven't," Josie said. Her snuffly voice struggled out through her tears. "You've made me so happy. I'd give you every penny I've got. You, Matthew and Gwynnie mean the world to me."

"You mean the world to us too."

"Then let's go and start cleaning the place up. I can face it now I know I never have to live there again."

"What cleaning stuff will we need?" Beth asked, sniffing away her tears.

"Nothing at all. I kept buying it when I was walking the town, knowing I'd got a big job ahead of me. I'm short of nothing, except the desire to go back and live there."

"I know," Beth said. "Matthew does, too."

The clean-up started in earnest that day. Josie found a new enthusiasm for the task. Beth, by nature a fastidious housekeeper, attacked the accumulated debris and waste with zeal.

"If we can clear away the rubbish, it won't take us many visits to have the place clean and tidy again," Beth said. "I guess we'll have to go to the tip a few times."

"Look at you. Clearing away my mess, and you a vicar's wife and an accountant. What a girl you are," Josie said.

Beth blushed, remembering the time when she thought she'd be helping Josie dispose of stolen goods. "You're my friend. My best friend."

"Bless you," Josie said. "I suppose I'll have to get a dealer in to clear my furniture. When we can finally see it."

"We might need it if we get an unfurnished place."

"You won't want my old stuff," Josie said.

"We'll be glad of it. Apart from the nursery equipment, we don't own a stick of furniture. We'll need something to sit on as well as beds to sleep in."

"My own daughter wouldn't have this stuff in her house when she moved away. She turned her nose up at it and bought new."

Beth smiled. "Matthew and I can't afford to buy new." She touched Josie's sideboard with tenderness. "We'll never be able to afford quality furniture like this."

She knew that had pleased Josie, because she gave her a rib-crushing hug. "Bless you," she said once again.

Beth's phone rang. She was expecting a call from Matthew to update them but was amazed to see it was her mother calling. She went into the hall to answer, unsure what to expect.

She soon re-joined Josie. "That was my dad. My parents are coming back from Portugal next month. Tom Grace has given notice on The Willows, and they want to sort everything out when he leaves."

"Will they want to stay with you?"

"They know we don't have room. They'll stay at The Willows."

"How long is it since you saw them?"

"The last time I visited them was five years ago. They don't know anything about what happened to me. They know about Matthew, but not how we met. They can't wait to see Gwynnie for the first time. They're a bit nervous about meeting Matthew because they're not church goers. I've told them I'm still not either, so they're not to worry."

"They'll love him. Everyone loves Matthew."

"I hope you're right," Beth said.

"Of course they will. Anyway, they're making the effort to see you at last. They must know you two can't afford to go flying off visiting them in Portugal," Josie said.

Beth knew she always said it as she saw it, and this time, she couldn't argue with her.

"Are they going to sell The Willows?"

"They didn't say. Time will tell. The way it always does."

Gwynnie was starting to grizzle. She had finally become bored with being confined to the small playpen. Beth picked her up. "You're going to meet your grandma and grandad," she said. "Won't that be nice?"

"And about time too," Josie said. "The child will be starting school soon."

Beth laughed. She knew her parents and their wanderlust ways all too well. Josie would never understand the way things are with us, she thought. It was ironic since Josie's daughter had moved away without giving her a second thought.

Matthew arrived home at around seven. He was weary, hungry, and full of news. He had spent all afternoon at the police station with Edward Hooper, popped back to the hospital to update Alison, and then headed home.

He told her what had happened, watching her alarm grow as the story unfolded.

Beth had known Alison had escaped virtually unhurt from a car accident, but he could see the news that it had been a murder attempt terrified her.

"Don't worry. Janos has been arrested," he said. "He'll appear in court tomorrow."

"They mustn't let him out," Beth said. "Alison will never be safe if he's at large."

"The police will oppose bail. He'll stay locked up."

Josie appeared with tea and sandwiches for Matthew and then joined them to hear the rest of the story.

Matthew took a grateful gulp of tea and bit hungrily into a sandwich. "Alison saw him in the mirror. He'd tailed her from Brooksley Hall." He was speaking with his mouth full, hungry yet anxious to tell the story.

"He was at the gala?" Beth asked.

"When security checked their CCTV recordings, they saw he'd been skulking about the shrubbery all evening. They'd only been watching the footage of the entrances and exits and the car park. There were some pricey motors parked there last night, so they prioritised those. The cameras picked up Alison leaving, and a couple of minutes later, they picked up Janos driving away."

Beth shivered. "She should have gone to the police when he threatened her," she said. "Why on earth didn't she have Ivan driving her last night?"

"Who knows? I don't think any of us suspected we were in any danger. Who'd have thought he'd do something so crazy? It was complete madness. He must have been eaten away with the desire for revenge. She'd hired the outside security people the venue uses. They're used to monitoring big occasions. She thought that would be better than Ivan's motley crew. God help her. She was only a couple of hundred yards from home when he struck."

"Poor Alison," Beth said. "Gemma did say he was bearing a grudge. I should have paid more attention."

"Me too. Anyway, Alison's now told the police everything and got Ivan to hand over the security footage from the factory of Janos threatening her."

Beth sighed. "Let's hope he gets a long sentence."

Matthew nodded. "He should do. I've been to the station with Edward Hooper, and he's reported the extortion. He's handed over his mobile, so they have the video of Gemma that Janos was blackmailing him with, and all the texts and invoices."

"Does Gemma know?"

"She was all in favour, but she didn't want the London incidents brought up. She said her stupidity meant he'd get away with those."

"Brave girl to accept responsibility," Josie said.

Matthew and Beth nodded. "She's certainly got guts," Matthew said.

"So, are we free of him at last?" Beth asked.

"It looks like it. I'm pretty sure he won't get bail. I just wish Alison and Edward had reported him in the first place, but Alison doesn't trust the police, and Edward was trying to protect Gemma."

Matthew went with Edward Hooper to court the next day to see Janos appear before the magistrate. Edward needed support but didn't want to put Diana through the ordeal of facing the man who had caused them so much pain, so he was glad to have Matthew with him.

The procedure was simple. Bail was refused and he was remanded in custody, awaiting trial in the Crown Court. Until it happened, neither had allowed themselves to believe it could all be over. Janos had been their nemesis, in and out of their lives for so long, creating heartache and havoc and always walking away unscathed.

He had stared hard at them from the dock, and Matthew could feel his seething resentment. He gave them one last vengeful look as he was led away to the cells. He sneered before turning his back and disappearing down the steps.

"I guess we're off his Christmas card list now," Matthew said, trying to make light of what had just chilled him to the bone.

"We're on his list for revenge forever, that's for sure."

Matthew detected fear in Edward's tone. "Alison is too," he said. "I'm glad she wasn't here today. Let's hope he gets a long sentence."

They walked back towards the car in silence. It was only when Matthew was driving away that Edward spoke.

"I never thought of myself as a violent man," he said, "but I would like to beat the sneer off that man's face. I'm ashamed to say that to you, a man of the cloth, but it's how I feel, and it eats me away."

"Someone hurt Beth a long time ago, and I felt exactly the same towards him," Matthew said. "It passed eventually. I never thought I could let the anger go, but real life knocked it out of me."

"Was that when you were stabbed?"

Matthew nodded. "Seeing Beth fight to get my life back on track put a lot of things in perspective, but I don't recommend such a drastic cure for you."

"It's good to remember that other people have had their troubles too," Edward said. "It's so easy to get bogged down in your own."

"Talking of troubles," Matthew said, "I get to meet my in-laws for the first time next month. They're coming over from Portugal to stay for a while."

"With you? Wherever will you put them?"

Matthew laughed. "They're staying at their old place. They plan to do some sorting out. On the bright side, they get to meet Gwynnie. I expect they'll be too busy with her to pay me much attention."

"You'll stand up to their scrutiny," Edward said. "Never doubt that."

The irony of Edward's words came to haunt Matthew for months. Beth's parents' visit started off well. He liked them immediately and he felt they were warming to him.

He was surprised at how weathered and worn they looked. Her mother had been in her early forties when baby Beth made her surprise appearance, and her father had just reached fifty. Since leaving the UK they had spent the last ten years in the open air, living either in Portugal or onboard their boat.

The sun and wind had coloured their skin to a deep chestnut brown, but instead of it glowing, it was dry and deeply wrinkled. They were still spritely. Their active lifestyle had kept them supple and strong, but there was no mistaking that here was a woman in her late sixties with a husband in his seventies.

They adored Gwynnie at first sight. She was at the responsive, cute stage of development where she was starting to chatter. They were warm and affectionate people and she responded to them enthusiastically.

He knew Beth was delighted to see them again and she was relieved he was getting on well with them. They were slightly awkward with him at first, but he was used to disarming apprehensive reactions. It came with his job.

They announced their plans for what they were calling their fourth age. They had sold their boat and they had vacated their villa and put it into the hands of a holiday letting agency. They were going to head to Australia, buy a Winnebago, and explore that country before heading over to New Zealand. After that, they had plans of island hopping in the Pacific.

Matthew found it hard to associate this outward thinking, adventurous couple with his shy and nervous wife. He had never known her before Wayne Jackson had changed her outlook on life forever.

He could tell her parents were finding Beth difficult to come to terms with. Her timidity and tentativeness seemed to perplex them. It was obvious she was unlike the daughter they had left behind. In the end he persuaded her to tell them what had happened to her to help them understand the change. Their anxiety was apparent in everything they said to her.

He watched them listen in amazement as she told of how she had been attacked, raped and left for dead.

She told her story in the most concise, unemotional way she could.

"Why didn't you tell us? We'd have come straight away," her mother said.

Matthew could see the sorrow that clouded her face and the tears that were forming,

"You couldn't have helped," she said. "I shut everyone out deliberately. I created a bubble and I retreated into it. I'd have stayed there for ever if it hadn't been for Matthew."

Her mother did not look convinced. "I'd have taken care of you."

"I wouldn't have let you. I wouldn't have agreed to see you. It was that bad. Matthew gradually broke the walls down with Josie's help. I resisted his efforts for a long time."

Her father looked at Matthew. "We had no idea how much we owed you," he said. "I'm so thankful."

They now knew the bare minimum of what Beth and Matthew had faced.

Matthew knew Beth had been selective in telling her story. She had not mentioned the scarring Jackson had left behind, and she hadn't mentioned Matthew's stabbing.

"You know now," Beth said, "and everything is fine. I never thought I'd let anyone get close to me again, but here I am. A wife and mother. It's miraculous, to be honest, so let's not dwell on the past. It does me no good."

He sensed they wanted to know more, and he prepared

himself to be the provider of answers to their questions. He knew Beth so well he was aware she had now locked the door on her story. She had said everything she wanted but would trust him to answer their questions from then on.

The questions came when he and Beth's mother took Gwynnie to the park. He was able to supply her with all the detail that Beth found too painful to face. She was aghast at what her daughter had been through, and she said she couldn't find the words to thank him.

"Do you think our girl will ever come back?' she asked.

"I don't know what your girl was like before all this happened. I wish I did. All I can say is that she is a tremendously strong woman in her own way. She's forged a new person out of the devastation of the past. I think that's all we can ask."

He went on to tell her about Beth's bravery as he had fought for his life after the stabbing, and how she had pushed his recovery forward in her own determined but gentle way.

"My God," she said. "What you two have been through. I don't know how Geoff and I will ever live with the guilt. We've been so selfish, all these years. We assumed Beth had our strong spirit and were totally convinced by her occasional upbeat messages."

"She made her choice, and she was perfectly happy with it. She wanted you to live the life you chose. She always says you gave her the best eighteen years she could have wanted, but she knows that life wasn't what you would have chosen. She wanted you to be free, Chris. She is the most selfless person I have ever met, and I can't tell you how much I love her."

"You don't need to tell me," she said. "I can feel it coming from your pores. You're just the same about Gwynnie. All in all, I couldn't wish for more for Beth. I just wish it could have happened in a different way."

Matthew nodded. "I can see what you mean, but I wouldn't change a thing. We were meant for each other."

"Like Geoff and me," she said. "I just hope you look after Gwynnie better than we managed to do for Beth. I'm pleased you're both happy now, but I'm going to have to carry a guilt that will never go away. Geoff too."

"Beth wouldn't want that."

"That's what makes it worse."

Chris and Geoff insisted on treating them to dinner. Matthew didn't want to go, and suspected Beth wasn't keen either, but neither wanted to disappoint them.

Feeling obliged, they accepted, and the next evening, they left Gwynnie with Josie and headed into town. The table was booked at Piccolino's, an expensive Italian restaurant.

They started to relax and feel glad they'd made the effort. The food was delicious, and despite the cold night outside, the place was so warm it would have been easy to imagine they had all met for dinner in Tuscany. Matthew, after all his apprehension, felt blessed to feel at ease with his in-laws.

Geoff cleared his throat. "Chris and I have made a decision. I can't tell you how deeply we feel about letting you go through all that alone, Beth."

Beth shook her head. "I didn't give you a choice. And I wasn't alone. Matthew found me and rescued me."

"It's good of you to say that, Beth, but you saying it won't make us feel any easier. Anyway, it's prompted us to do something we should have done when we left you behind, all those years ago. You seemed so self-assured back then we allowed ourselves to forget you were little more than a child. We realise now we've totally abandoned you for years."

"I don't see it like that. I knew you would always be there for me, but you two were always footloose. You needed to follow your own path. You'd tied yourselves down for eighteen years to give me a stable home. As I grew up, I could see that life was stifling you both. I knew the life you craved wasn't for me."

"That's gracious of you. We knew you were a homebird, not like us two restless souls, and we made that our excuse for leaving you behind," Chris said. "Time to make things right. We've been to the solicitors and we're transferring The Willows over to you and Gwynnie. You always loved that house."

More than you'll ever know, Matthew thought as the memory of how it helped her recovery drifted into his mind.

"Are you sure you want to do that?" Beth asked.

"Totally," Geoff said. "It will be in a trust. We have to face it, we're getting on now. We have to make sure you'll be financially secure when we've gone. It's time to put things in order."

The atmosphere at the table changed. A sombre and reflective mood engulfed what had been a happy table. Matthew knew Beth did not want or need reminding of the mortality of her parents. He'd watched her getting used to having them around and now she looked stricken by the thought of losing them permanently.

"That's a wonderful thing to do," Matthew said.

As soon as they had revealed their plan his mind had been in overdrive. It was such an amazing opportunity to create a project for him and Beth to work on. His face started to beam as ideas poured into his head. "We could convert it into a rehab centre." He was on a roll. "Even better, a women's refuge. Can you imagine how safe the women would feel, and the garden would be perfect for the children. We will be able to do so much good."

He spoke from his kind and honest heart. He had no need for big houses, but he had a burning desire to help anyone in need. He always assumed people who got on with him knew how he thought and could share his vision.

He registered Beth's parents' mood changing. It went from the reflective way they'd contemplated the aging process to an icy chill.

"You misunderstand us, Matthew," said Geoff. "We want to give Beth a beautiful home to bring Gwynnie up in. We're not making a charitable endowment to your good causes."

Matthew blushed. "I'm so sorry. You must think I'm rude. Beth and I have been so committed to helping the disadvantaged it was the first thing that occurred to me."

"It occurs to me that whilst you crusade for the underprivileged, as is your right, I see our daughter and granddaughter on their way to joining their ranks."

Matthew heard the anger in his voice. He reeled. He couldn't believe what he'd just heard. He and Beth had a warm and loving home and it had never crossed his mind that they were in need of anything.

"I'm so sorry you feel that way," he said. He felt Beth's hand grasp his arm reassuringly, but this time it didn't work. He was not reassured. He was a mass of confusion. He couldn't fathom why it had all gone so wrong. It had seemed such an obvious opportunity to do good. "It never occurred to me we lacked anything. Obviously, we need a bigger place for Josie to stay with us, but we don't need a mansion."

"The Willows is a lovely family home, not a mansion. No matter how dedicated you are to good causes, Matthew, your family deserves a decent home. I thought you'd see that." Chris spoke with sadness.

"I thought we'd got one," he said, totally mortified.

"We have," Beth said.

He saw the dismay on her face as she watched her parents looking annoyed.

"We all need to step back and think about this. It is the most wonderfully kind thing to want to do for us," Beth finally said.

He knew she was, in her subtle way, trying to smooth things over. He didn't want to be the one to suggest leaving. It would have looked as if he was being petulant, so he was grateful when Beth said they had to be getting back.

"We hate leaving Gwynnie," she said, "even for a couple of hours."

"You've made your point, Beth. You are a wonderful mother, and I wasn't. I should never have left you back then," Chris said.

Matthew felt Beth's pain. He knew that was not what she had meant.

CHAPTER NINE

The journey home from Piccolino's was uncomfortable. For the first time since they had met, Beth found herself at odds with Matthew. She had known at once that she would have loved to have moved into the Willows and brought Gwynnie up there.

She could imagine Gwynnie taking over the garden shed that had once been her own special den. She could imagine her on the old swing that hung from the apple tree. She could imagine Josie living on the top floor, independent but still part of the family.

She had never experienced dreams like these, but they had leapt into her mind as soon as she had heard of her parents' plan. She loved everything she could possibly imagine about returning to The Willows, and nothing about these thoughts centred on the worth of the property. It was all about the life that lovely old house offered them.

She knew instinctively that Matthew's objections would all be focused on not missing the opportunity to do good. He would hate the idea of living in a large house when it could be put to better use. She loved him for his integrity and the strength of his principles, but her primary focus was on their family and their life together. It struck her that she and Gwynnie might be taking second place in his priorities.

"I think I put my foot in it with your parents," he said at last.

"They made that clear," she said, and then regretted her directness. "They were only thinking of Gwynnie and me."

"And I'm not?" he said.

Beth knew then they had a real problem. He was a good man, the best she had ever known. He was being true to himself and his conscience. The only way to preserve peace was for her to let things lie.

"You always think of us," she replied. "I know that." It was the best she could do. She wanted nothing to come between them and she could see The Willows becoming a problem. "I might be wrong, but I don't think they would proceed if we were to turn it into a refuge."

"As you said, they made that clear. But I did spring it on them." He fell into silence. "They might see what a great opportunity it offers when they've thought about it."

"I'd rather do without The Willows than it become an issue between us," Beth said after an uncomfortable pause.

"I'd rather turn it to good use. It's got such great potential. If we can't do that, I'd sooner turn it down. It won't be an issue, we don't need a fancy house. We've got each other. We'll always have a loving home."

"It's so sad that such a kind and well-intentioned offer has become such a bone of contention," she said. "We need to give everything a lot of thought." She thought it best to buy time for them all, then said no more. She felt totally wretched. They were, after all, looking for a larger property to rent and were prepared to take a contribution from Josie to make that possible. Her parents had offered them a perfect solution. She sighed. She was tired and she knew she couldn't think clearly. There was a good chance she'd express herself badly and upset Matthew even more. They had never had a serious disagreement, and she wanted to keep it that way.

Matthew re-opened the conversation as soon as they were snuggled together in bed. "Can you imagine the benefit of turning The Willows into a women's refuge? It would be perfect. The women and children would feel so safe in the village."

She saw at once Matthew's reasoning was locked in.

"Maybe you can persuade your parents to see that. I guess they'd hate the idea of a rehab centre."

"They definitely would," Beth said, glad to be able to agree on something. "We all need time. I know my parents are feeling guilty now they know what happened to me and they want to make amends for not being around. They don't understand how I deliberately kept everything from them. I wanted to protect them. I don't need The Willows as compensation."

"They don't know you all that well if they think you do. You always put others first," he said.

"You certainly do," she said out loud. You put them before Gwynnie and me, she thought, shutting all dreams of an idyllic family life at The Willows from her mind.

"I'm going to call on Alison before I go into the office," Matthew said. "I want to see for myself how she's getting on. She always says she's fine when I call her."

"Give her my love," Beth said. "Ask her if she's up to a visit from Gwynnie and me."

"I will." He kissed her and left, knowing that they had both been on edge that morning, so he had purposely avoided any mention of The Willows.

He was brooding on the problem as he drove to Alison's. He felt The Willows would allow him to work with Beth to do something amazing. So often, victims of domestic abuse who came to the centre were trapped because they didn't want to drag their children off to emergency accommodation in some run-down bed and breakfast. He could see how safe they would feel at The Willows and what a great place it would be for them to escape to with their children. He could envisage working with her on the project. Her sensitivity would be such an asset.

He would ask her to talk to her parents to help them understand how perfect it would be for them all. He couldn't think of a better project to bring them all together.

Alison looked her usual confident self when she opened the door. "I'm glad you came this morning," she said. "I'm going into the office this afternoon. I can't sit about on my fat ass any longer."

He followed her into the kitchen.

"Coffee?" she asked.

"Please," he said. "Now tell me how you really are whilst you make it. I think you're rushing back to work." He knew her so well he could see through her forced cheerfulness.

"Maybe. I still feel like shit," she said. "It's really hit me that I came so close to meeting my maker and I've realised I'm just not ready. But keep that to yourself. That's why I want to get back. It will stop me brooding."

"Don't you think you need to talk it through with someone? It was one hell of a close call."

She threw back her head and laughed. "Do you really think I'd see a shrink? This is me. Alison. You're the closest I'll ever get to talking it through with someone."

They took their coffee through to the sitting room.

"I have been thinking things over. Something like that makes you realise you have to make things count."

"So, what have you decided?"

She sighed heavily. "I don't have anybody looking out for me except Ivan. I'm going to throw my lot in with Brooksie."

"You're going to marry him?"

"I'm not sure. He comes with so much baggage from his previous marriages. There are kids of his crawling out from the woodwork from his brief encounters too. They all want their share of his pie. They have no idea it's a pie with no filling, poor sods."

Matthew frowned, unsure of what she meant by throwing her lot in with him.

"He's moving in here. We're going to see how things go, but we are going into business together. His pile, Brooksley Hall, is falling to bits. We're going to renovate it and upgrade it. He's already operating it as a hotel and an events venue. We can create a health centre and spa there too. Our lawyers are working out the legal stuff. He needs my backing to get it done up because he's stony broke. I need his address book and connections to make it work. The gala was a bit of an experiment to see how we work together."

"You kept that quiet," he said. He frowned. "Your answer to your close encounter with death is to take on more work and make more money?"

"You certainly tell it how it is," she said. "Actually, I want him here. I want to wake up with someone beside me. I want there to be someone here when I hear a noise in the night. I want someone to cook for. I'm also tired of working my ass off on my own. That's why I've enjoyed our collaboration, Matthew. The trouble is, you don't want to make money, you just want to spend mine. I need to keep earning to do that. I want a partner, an equal, to bounce ideas off, like I do with you. I'm just not sure I want to become his third wife and inherit a horde of grasping stepchildren. That's how he talks of them. I just want him here, in my bed and in the boardroom. If we approach it like a business, I know I can cope. His lawyers can protect their interests and mine will look after me."

Matthew reflected on what she had said. "You're scared of being alone," he said.

"Okay, Sigmund, you've got it. I'm bloody terrified. I've worked my ass off and here I am, three dead husbands later, completely alone. He worships me and I like him being around. I'm just not sure I want to marry him. Husband number four? It would be a joke. People would think I'd finally slept my way to the top and got myself a title."

"When have you been scared of what people say?"

"Never, because it never mattered. Most of what they said was true and I didn't care. Water off a duck's back. This matters."

"Alison, I think you already know you're in love," he said, "and I think you're scared to admit it."

"How the hell do I know what being in love feels like? I've never been in love. I've just married to claw my way out of the gutter and up the greasy pole. Now I've just had a near death experience. I might be being irrational."

"That's something you'll never be," he said. "Although I still think you should have gone to the police in the first place. I never thought dealing with him yourself was a sensible decision."

"Well, thank you, Father Matthew, for your in-depth analysis and critique. If you breathe a word of any of what I've said, I'll have your balls on a plate. Anyway, you look like you've lost a shilling and found a penny. What's up with you?"

"How long have you got?" He explained about The Willows and his dream of turning it into a refuge. He became more and more animated as he talked, seeing the enormous potential of the project.

"And what does Beth think?" Alison asked when he had finished.

He looked at her in puzzlement. "I haven't asked, but she'll be on board. She always is," he said. He paused. It occurred to him he should have asked her what she thought. The refuge made such perfect sense it hadn't crossed his mind.

"I know Beth married a saint, but you need to come down off your cloud occasionally. What if she wants a nice home for Gwynnie to grow up in?"

"We'll always give her a nice home," he protested.

"You'll always make sure she has a roof over her head, I grant you that."

"I don't want her growing up thinking having stuff matters."

"So says the man whose wife had to borrow a dress and get her shoes from a charity shop to go to a gala. A wife who tried to get out of it at first because she didn't have anything to wear."

"Things like that don't matter to Beth and me."

"Have you ever asked her?"

"She knew who I was and what I stood for from the start," he said. He was feeling awkward.

"Oh, Father Matthew, so wise and yet so foolish. I went to Sunday School, you know. I know all about how hard it is for a rich man to get into heaven. My lousy father sent me so he could beat my poor mother up without me seeing it. You'll slip through the eye of that needle easily enough, but be careful you're not making Beth and Gwynnie your beasts of burden, the camels who carry you there."

"That's not fair," he said, inwardly cringing at the metaphor she'd used from the bible.

"Isn't it? This conversation started with you saying you'd not asked her how she felt." Alison sighed. "Matthew, I know I'm lucky to be rich, but I try to give back. If I didn't have my business, I wouldn't be able to help your centres. I want Brooksie and me to work together on them. I'm hoping to squeeze my fat ass, and his, through the eye of that needle one day."

"You think I live on a cloud?"

"Your head is usually in the clouds. You don't see what's in front of your nose."

Matthew looked at Alison with respect. This was a woman who could tell the truth as she saw it without rancour. She was also a woman who was comfortable in her own skin. She knew who she was, flaws and all. He'd always thought the same to be true of him. Now he wasn't so sure.

His mood altered as he drove to the office. He reviewed his mental planning for refurbishing The Willows and turning it into a refuge. He started to consider what Beth might be thinking. He knew The Willows had been instrumental in her fight back to recovery. Could she possibly be thinking of making their home there?

He called Edward Hooper as soon as he got to his desk. He arranged to meet him for a drink that night. He'd sound him out. Edward was a family man above everything else. It would be good, he decided, to hear what he thought.

Beth and Josie were heading off to Josie's house. The clean-up operation was going well, and it was fully understood that Beth and Matthew were going to find a larger place and Josie would move in with them permanently. Josie knew they'd been looking but hadn't found anything in their price range.

"There was a bit of an atmosphere at breakfast," Josie said. "I've never known you two so edgy with each other."

"We've got a lot on our minds. My parents announced last night that they want to sign The Willows over to Gwynnie and me. They're selling everything else up and going on one last big adventure."

"About time they did something for you, girl," Josie replied. "It would make a lovely home for you all. That's great news."

"There'd be plenty of room for you too," Beth said. She sighed heavily. "Anyway, it might not happen, so it's no good dreaming."

"Why ever not?"

"Matthew wants to turn it into a women's refuge or a rehab centre. I don't think my parents will go ahead if he digs his heels in."

"Is he crazy? Doesn't he want a lovely home for his family?"

"Not if it could be put to better use," Beth said.

"What better use could there be than a home for the three of you?"

Beth winced. "I can see his point." Loyalty was second nature to her.

"And I can see yours. You can't always put yourself last, girl. Have you told him what you think?"

"No," Beth said. "I'm thinking about whether I should. We've never had a serious difference of opinion before, and I'd hate it to become a problem."

"It sounds as if it already is a problem. You just want to hide it from him," Josie said. "Don't you think the good Lord put the idea in your parents' heads for a reason?"

"I never thought of it like that," Beth said. "It's an interesting thought. Anyway, I doubt they'd go ahead on his terms, so it will all come to nothing. Let's not talk about it anymore. Let's concentrate on getting your place shipshape."

Matthew was uncommunicative when he got back from the office. It cut Beth to the heart to be on the receiving end of short, sharp answers. She had never known him to be like that. She assumed he felt his dream of a women's refuge would come to nothing.

She wasn't ready to talk about The Willows, but she did want to know how Alison was getting on. All she learnt was that she was fine and returning to work. The terseness of the replies didn't ease her anxiety.

Josie didn't chatter as much as she usually did over dinner, Gwynnie was playing up and was refusing her food and Matthew was just pushing his round his plate. Beth felt completely at a loss and concentrated on trying to tempt the grumpy little child into eating.

"Beth! She clearly doesn't want any more," Matthew said.

Beth winced at his snappy irritability.

"I'll take her up for an early bath. I'm meeting up with

Edward at half seven at The Blacksmith's Arms, so I need to get a move on." He got up and lifted Gwynnie from her high-chair. "I'll call you when she's ready for bed."

Beth wiped a tear from the corner of her eye as she watched him go upstairs. It felt so unjust for him to be so cross. Her parents had wanted to do something nice for her, and he was escalating it into a major crisis.

"I think I'll tell my parents to forget it," she said to Josie. "It's just not worth it."

"Then you're a fool," Josie said. "At least talk it over with him properly first."

"He doesn't seem to be in the mood for talking. I've never known him be like this."

Matthew was angry with himself. He couldn't explain quite why. He had expected Beth to back him immediately over The Willows, but he knew he wasn't angry with her. He'd felt troubled since his talk with Alison. Up until then everything had seemed so straightforward. Turning The Willows into a women's refuge was such a great opportunity for them to do something good together that he'd got carried away with the idea. He'd felt like a child on Christmas Eve, the possibilities were so exciting.

He was so used to agreement and harmony from Beth he'd never considered she might think differently. Alison had made him start to think it was a possibility, but Beth had still said nothing except they needed time to think. He hoped Edward would help clear his thoughts.

They sat in their usual corner, the place where Edward had so often confided in Matthew in the past.

"You look as if you've got the weight of the world on your back," Edward observed. "Is it my time to provide the shoulder to cry on?"

Matthew didn't smile. "I'm not looking for sympathy. I

need your objectivity," he said. "You're a family man down to your bones."

"I do my best."

"Beth's parents want to put their place in West Stanton into trust for Beth and Gwynnie."

"That's wonderful," Edward said without hesitating.

"It's a big old place, far too grand for us."

"I know the one. It's where Oliver Hargreaves used to live. It was all over the news a couple of years ago. It'd make a lovely family home."

"Says the man who lives in a mansion," Matthew replied. "Oh. I'm sorry, Edward." He was aware it had sounded crass and petulant, and he could tell Edward had been hurt by his remark. He tried to add a context. "It's a great big place, too showy for us."

"Actually, I said that as your friend. I support your good deeds in every way I can, whether I live in a mansion or not."

Matthew knew he was signalling his hurt and regretted his words even more.

"Have you and Beth discussed this?" Edward asked.

"No. She said she needs time to think. I guess she has to decide if she wants to try to persuade her folks to change their mind. I can't see why anyone would object to the idea. It's a no-brainer. It's the perfect place to provide a safe, healing environment for those women."

Edward took a long drink from his pint glass. "Objectivity, you said?"

Matthew nodded.

"I know you'd be happy to be as poor as a church mouse for the rest of your days. You're turning your back on a lovely home for you and your family. I know you're looking for a bigger place so Josie can stay on. This would be the perfect answer."

"We don't need anything that grand," Matthew said.

Edward looked at Matthew and shook his head. "Matt,

you've done the *sickness and health* thing far more than any couple I know. You've both been through it, and you've always looked out for each other. Now you're facing the *for richer for poorer* part. Good grief, you've done the poorer bit. At least Beth has. She's having to drive round in that old death trap of yours and she had to borrow Diana's frock to go to the gala. Doesn't she deserve a nice home? You won't be able to provide for Gwynnie's future, but her grandparents are trying to do just that. You're standing in their way. You won't have a fat pension coming your way. Diana would have signed the papers by now if she was in Beth's place, I can tell you that as a fact."

Matthew felt as if the breath had been punched out of him. It was his turn to take a long drink. As he did so, Edward continued his assault.

"You're the kindest, most honest man I've ever met," Edward said. "You're far cleverer than me, but sometimes you are stupid. You can't seriously want to deprive Beth and Gwynnie of a lovely home so you can follow your own compulsion to live in poverty and do good?"

"Is that what I'm doing?"

"Yes, in my objective opinion. It may not be what you wanted to hear, but you did ask."

"You're the second person to say that to me today."

"Strange we both said the same thing, don't you think? If you need to ask for opinions, you're not as certain as you think you are. Are you asking my permission to carry on fighting to create a refuge, or are you asking me what I think?"

"I was asking what you think," Matthew said, "and you've not held back. Maybe I assumed you'd agree with me."

"Then my work here is done. In my opinion, you'd be punishing your wife and child to pursue your own agenda. I hope you're thinking it through properly at last, and not just knee-jerking to your usual sack cloth and ashes conclusion."

"Is that what I do?"

"You did ask," Edward said. "Over this, it looks as if you want to keep Beth and Gwynnie in sack cloth too."

He sighed. "Let's have another drink."

Matthew walked the long way home. He had a lot to think about. Alison and Edward had been so emphatic he had to reconsider. He realised he had forgotten one thing completely. Edward had been correct in what he'd said — his reaction to Beth's parents' offer had been a knee-jerk one. He'd not given it any thought, but just blurted out his ready-made philanthropic vision. Working for the charity had made him myopic. He'd not bothered to ask for Beth's opinion.

He plunged his hands into his pockets and frowned. His fingers found the heavy keys that lay in the farthest depth of his pocket. He turned immediately in the direction of the church. *I'll talk to the Boss. That's what I should have done in the first place.*

It was a difficult evening for Beth. It was so strange to process that Matthew had taken himself off to the pub to meet with Edward.

He's turned to drink rather than talk to me.

He always spent his evenings with her and Josie unless he had to deal with work issues. Combined with his distanced behaviour, it not only hurt, it created a puzzle she couldn't solve. Were she and Gwynnie so easy to overlook? She had no wish to talk it over with Josie. It was too painful.

Josie had gone up to bed at ten as she always did. Beth waited until eleven before going upstairs. She had just turned off the bedroom light when she heard Matthew return. He made his way straight up to bed. He was clearly trying not to disturb her, but he was bumping into things in the darkness. She heard a repressed *ouch* just before he climbed in beside her. She could detect the smell of beer but had no idea how much he'd drunk that night. She lay still and feigned sleep.

She could tell Matthew could not sleep. She was aware of him tossing and turning beside her. He sighed each time he turned, and it became impossible to maintain the pretence of sleep.

She put on the bedside light and blinked at its brightness. "What's troubling you?" she asked. She felt his arms slip round her and she breathed a little easier after he'd given her the familiar gentle squeeze.

"Everything. I've received some home truths today and I'm struggling," he said.

"The Willows?"

"Yes. As you said, we needed time to think."

"I've done my thinking," she said, suddenly decisive. "I'd like to live there. I'd like Gwynnie to grow up there. I'm not prepared for it to come between us, so it doesn't have to happen, but I'm sure my parents won't just sign it over to your charity." She took a deep breath. "You need to know I'm not prepared to try to persuade them. I just can't help you give away what's rightfully Gwynnie's."

There was silence. Beth felt her face burning. She didn't know what her honesty would provoke, and she was terrified that it would place barriers between them. She became acutely aware that her heart was pounding as she waited for his reply.

She was aware his face was nuzzling her neck and she pulled away, annoyed.

Surely, he's not using that to persuade me.

"I was just trying to let you know how much I love you," he said..

Beth's bravery exceeded even her expectations. "But do you love me more than your constant need to help the disadvantaged? I thought we meant more to you than anything."

"Don't you see that's what tears me apart? I'm scared I love you more than I love God," he said. "I made vows."

"You made vows to me too," she said. "Did you mean them?"

"I can't believe you could even ask, yet that's what Edward asked me too," he said.

"Then he's a wise man," she replied. "I think you need to decide if you can have us in your life and still sleep easy with your conscience."

"I thought we were talking about The Willows."

"We are. We're also talking about us," she said. "It hurts me that you'd take security away from Gwynnie and me and give it away. I'm sorry if you think that makes me greedy or wicked."

She wasn't capable of saying more. She turned the light out, moved to the edge of her side of the bed and tried to fall asleep. It took hours.

When she woke, she saw Matthew was sitting up in bed looking at her. What struck her was the tenderness of his look — it was full of love. It reassured her.

"Good morning," he said. "You realise you've just spent the night with a complete idiot." He stretched out his arm, inviting her to curl against him. She moved closer and rested her head against him, hopeful they could reach an understanding.

"I do that every night," she said, "but you're my idiot and I love you. I can't stand the way things have been between us." She was trying to normalise things after the intensity of the previous evening, taking her lead from what he'd said.

"You do know that you and Gwynnie are the most important things in my life?"

"I'm not sure I like being called a thing, but I've always known we're important to you. But are we important enough? Can we actually talk this Willows thing through now? I know I said we needed time to think, but you just seemed to put up the shutters and it's been awful. I've told you what's hurt me, and it nearly broke my heart to have to admit I want to safeguard it for Gwynnie. I didn't want you to think I'm not satisfied with what we have."

"I know. Tell me what you want to do," he said. "And tell me what you really want, not what you think I want to hear."

"I want to move there and make a permanent home for us. I'm happy to hold fundraisers in the garden, host training weekends for your volunteers and use the house to support you in any way we can think of, but I can't turn my back on that place. I love it too much."

He tightened his arm round her to give her a hug. "You're still thinking of me and my work," he said, "even though I didn't give you a second thought. I don't deserve you."

"What's changed your mind about the house?"

"Home truths delivered by people I respect. Alison and Edward gave it to me straight."

"Why could you talk to them and not to me?"

There was a pause and Beth felt concern building up inside her.

He seemed to be struggling to find the words. He opened his mouth to speak a couple of times and then closed it. The delay made her feel worse.

Eventually he spoke. "I assumed that you would automatically want what I wanted. It never occurred to me that you'd have your own ideas. It all seemed so blatantly obvious to me that night. I expected you to see it too. I could see why you'd not want a drug and alcohol rehab place, but I was positive you'd want to make it a women's refuge. I was convinced you'd be happy forever in whatever place we could find to rent."

Beth pulled away. "You think I want it because it's big and grand?"

Matthew shook his head. "No. I know you want to build our home there. I know it's where you feel secure. I know you love it. I just thought you'd automatically see it my way and back me up. I thought you'd persuade your parents to change their minds. I was being selfish and stupid."

"It was stupid to think they'd simply give it to you because you asked for it. I'm sorry, but I wouldn't have tried to persuade them to hand it over. I didn't think it was a fair thing to ask, and I knew I'd have been wasting my time."

"Like I said, I was being stupid."

It wasn't proving an easy conversation for Beth. She didn't want him to think she was being materialistic, and she didn't want him to go against his conscience. "I wanted you to see what a wonderful home we could make there, and how we could use it to do good." She hoped he would see that.

"You don't need to explain, Beth. You aren't capable of being selfish. You were just thinking of us, and Josie. I have tunnel vision sometimes. I just didn't look at it from your point of view. I didn't even allow you to have one because I expected you to go along with what I wanted. I've learned a lot about myself these last couple of days."

She started to feel a little easier. He seemed to understand how she felt. "So, what do you want us to do?"

"I want to apologise to your parents. I behaved like I was entitled to take their family home for my own schemes. I want to make it right with you because I'd got into the habit of assuming you didn't need anything nice in your life. I'd never questioned you might not want to have to borrow Diana's clothes or find shoes in a charity shop."

"I think I look pretty good in recycled chic." She smiled. "You know I'm not interested in having stuff. I didn't pine for a new outfit. But I do want a forever home with you and Gwynnie."

"Shall we talk to your parents and make it happen?"

"That would be wonderful, but what about the refuge? Have you abandoned that idea?"

"No, but I see now it's down to me to work to get one and not expect one to be handed over on a plate by people who don't even know me."

"I'll help you get one," Beth said, snuggling in again. "I'll go and see Mum and Dad this afternoon. It's time to make things right and get some closure."

"It's time for me to make things right," he said," with you and them. I should see them first. They must think I'm a complete . . ."

"Idiot," Beth finished his sentence. "Let's leave it at that."

CHAPTER TEN

Beth knew bridges had to be built between Matthew and her parents. It wasn't so she could get her hands on The Willows, it was because it mattered to her that they weren't seeing him as he really was. She knew he was going to apologise after work, but she thought she'd do some groundwork first.

Things were clear in her mind now. She'd always known she wanted to accept their offer, but she had needed things sorted between her and Matthew first.

They were glad to see her but were cautious in their welcome. The evening at Piccolino's had been uncomfortable and they were unsure of what message she'd arrived with.

"I've come to tell you we're both really sorry about the way we reacted the other night," she said, determined to address the issue immediately. "I should have accepted there and then, and Matthew should have been overcome with gratitude. He's mortified about how he reacted. I wanted you to know he'll be calling in on his way home from work to apologise."

She set Gwynnie on the floor and put her little bag beside her. She unpacked it and settled her to play with her toys and read her books.

"Before you say anything, Beth, we won't be handing this place over to your husband. We've talked it over and we agree. This house is for you and Gwynnie. It's high time we did something for you, especially now we know what you've been through." Her father sounded anxious, as though he was expecting an argument. "We're definitely not donating it to his charity."

"It's okay, Dad," Beth said reassuringly. "Matthew is really sorry about the way he reacted. He's heart and soul into making the world a better place and he gets carried away." She could see neither of her parents looked reassured.

"We can't understand why you and this baby girl of yours aren't at the top of his list of priorities." Her mother was frowning.

"We are, Mum. We truly are," Beth said. "He's got such a big heart that he wants to help everyone, and he never thinks of himself."

"It looks as if he never thinks of you two either," her father said. "We're not impressed."

It was heart-breaking for Beth to have to defend him to her parents. She wanted them to see him through her eyes. He was the kindest, most caring man she had ever known. The problem was, he'd hurt her for the first time ever by taking her for granted the way he had, and the wounds were still sore.

"He's programmed to think of others," Beth said. "He just forgets not everyone is as . . ."

"Good as him? He's a bit too full of his own saintliness, if you ask me." Her dad sounded bitter.

"No. He's really sweet and humble. He sees things every day that we can't even begin to imagine, and he wants to solve everyone's problems. It's hard for him to switch off. Please remember, he saved me from oblivion and has eased me back to life. Without him, I'd still be staring into space in that dreadful psychiatric hospital."

"We know. He was there for you when we weren't. You're not making this any easier for us, Beth." Her father sighed. "You didn't exactly give us chance to help. Can you imagine how we feel right now?"

It was her fault that they had been shut out of her

nightmare. Knowing she truly believed they wouldn't have been able to pull her from that abyss wasn't going to make them feel any better. She saw they were consumed with a guilt that they didn't deserve.

She took a long breath. "After it happened, I was terrified of any human touch, even yours. I accepted I'd never have children of my own. Matthew helped me rebuild my life. and now we have the child I never dreamed possible. I know it's hard for you to understand, but you couldn't have helped me on that journey. He helped me to stand on my own feet again when the doctors couldn't get through to me. All I ever wanted was my own child, but I was even scared of my own shadow. He showed me I could trust him, and I do. Now we're a family. And I want us to have the wonderful home you're offering us. He does, too. He's accepted we can have a good home without compromising his conscience."

"That's very big of him," her father said, still unconvinced. "And you should have turned to us. We'd have understood and been there for you."

"I didn't want you to know what that man did to me. I didn't want to explain to you that I was terrified of intimacy and yet I longed for a family. I couldn't tell you that I was never going to let a man touch me. It was too hard for me to face, let alone say, so I shut it out. Matthew helped me overcome all that by loving me without asking for a thing in return."

"So now it's payback and he'd like The Willows?" he said.

Beth flinched, distressed her dad wasn't listening, even though she was baring her soul.

Her mother moved over to her and put her arms around her. "I get it," she said. "He's done what we never could." She squeezed Beth tight.

"Mum, I trust him with every fibre of my body. He's my best friend, my lover, my husband, and the father of my little girl. And he's human, and sometimes, in wanting to help everyone he sees, he gets it wrong. He got this wrong and he's sorry. I just want you to believe that he's a good man. The best man you'll ever meet."

"That's actually your father," her mother said with a smile, trying to ease the tension in her husband, "but I'm sure Matthew is as wonderful as you say. We all got wrong-footed. If he saved you after all that you went through, we can make an effort to get to know him properly." She turned to face Geoff directly. "And he's given us the granddaughter we might never have had."

"Dad?" Beth asked, hoping he was coming round.

Her father scooped Gwynnie into his arms and dropped a soft kiss on her baby curls. "I'll try. Anything for my girls. All three of them."

Matthew felt uncomfortable as he drove over to The Willows after work. He was aware that Beth had already visited but was still unsure of the reception he'd face. He knew he deserved a frosty welcome after the way he'd leapt on the chance to turn their lovely home into a refuge. Not only that, he'd ridden roughshod over Beth in the attempt. His only concern was how to make it right between them.

Geoff was not welcoming. "You'd better come in," he said.

Matthew knew it was said begrudgingly. He followed him through to the kitchen he knew so well from the days when Beth had worked as a nanny there.

"Hello Matthew." Chris' welcome sounded more positive. "Sit down. We were just having a cup of tea. Shall I pour one for you?"

He felt it would have been graceless to refuse, even though he wanted to get on with his apology, so he replied, "White, no sugar please," and took a seat.

There was a pause as Chris fetched a cup and saucer and poured his tea.

He said thank you and then plunged in. There was no point delaying what he had to say. "I've come to apologise to you both. I behaved like an ungrateful idiot and I'm truly sorry." He felt Geoff looking at him with loathing and his courage wavered. He took a deep breath and ploughed on. "First of all, I need you to know that Beth and Gwynnie are more important to me than my life. I would die for them."

Chris smiled across at him, but Geoff's stony expression did not soften.

"So you thought you'd rob them of their rightful inheritance? A funny way of showing it," he said.

Matthew lowered his head for a moment. He was aware his actions could be interpreted that way. He took another deep breath. "Of course not." He knew that wasn't a helpful thing to say.

"We are waiting for an explanation," Geoff said, "because it seems to me you'd be happy for our daughter to carry on living in poverty."

"I can see why you would think that, but it isn't true, and to be fair, we don't live in poverty. We just don't have very much. I can see now I had things out of perspective. Some very good friends have pointed that out to me in the last few days. I was taking Beth for granted because she's always so sweet and kind. She's supported me in everything I've done, and I just assumed she'd see things my way."

"I'd like to understand what your way is, Matthew." Chris's voice sounded encouraging.

"I always want to make a difference. I want to make people's lives better. I took this job on to do that. I know it will always be low paid and that I'll never be able to give Beth and Gwynnie much more than a comfortable roof over their heads. I see so much poverty and suffering every day that I count our blessings. Compared to the people I work with, we've got it made. I try to find answers for them. The new centre we've just set up has been inundated with people needing support to get off drugs and women trying to escape from abuse. All that started to take over my thinking. I'm ashamed to say I never gave my own family a single thought when you made your offer. I didn't think of your feelings, either. I just saw a ready-made solution to one of the problems tormenting me, and I acted thoughtlessly. At that moment, I truly thought The Willows was heaven sent." That was the best explanation he could offer for his impulsive reaction.

"What's changed your mind?" Geoff asked.

"Shame. I'm ashamed of the way I treated you and Beth. I didn't even ask you what you thought. I was prepared to rob my wife and daughter of their birth right without even talking it through with Beth. It's no defence, but I got carried away."

"We hoped to help you be free to go on saving the world whilst you and your family live in a comfortable home. We know you and Beth will always have to scratch along on your salary, and we accept that. We were just trying to provide our daughter and granddaughter with some long-term security. There'll be no golden handshake for you when you grow old, no fat pension. We imagined we would be making it easier for you to carry on with your crusades whilst making sure Beth and Gwynnie are provided for."

"You make me feel even more ashamed," Matthew said. He hoped they could see his sincerity. "When I finally got off my high horse and discussed it with Beth, I found out she yearned to have a lovely home for Gwynnie to grow up in. She could also see how that wonderful home could support me in my . . . crusades." He used their term. "So, I'm here to say I'm sorry. I'm here to say I behaved thoughtlessly. But, most of all, to thank you for thinking of my family's future when I wasn't."

Chris was nodding. Matthew felt she was convinced he was being sincere.

"The Willows will be nothing to do with you," continued Geoff. "Your name will not be on the deeds. It will be protected for Beth and Gwyneth forever. You won't be able to work on Beth to change her mind in the years to come."

"Geoff," Chris said.

Matthew heard reproach in her tone.

"This man didn't hesitate to stake a claim on what we worked for all those years. I'm not prepared to sugar coat it."

"I don't want you to. I want you to have total peace of mind. I want you to see I love my wife and daughter with all my heart. I'm even more aware how much they matter to me since all this happened. I'm sorry you saw me acting in such a blinkered way. My friends ripped those blinkers off without mercy. Beth managed to widen my view even further, in a much kinder way."

"I'd have liked to have ripped your head off, let alone your blinkers." Geoff said, but this time there was the trace of a smile on his lips. "Shall we agree you made a complete prat of yourself, thinking I'd sign my house over to your junkies and battered wives, and deprive Beth and my own grand-daughter of their inheritance? But I hope you can see how bad we feel about letting her down in the past. We need to make sure her future is secure. Shall we be able to move past this?"

"I think we agree on everything," Matthew said. "I'm truly sorry, and I'm grateful you were prepared to hear me out."

"You can tell Beth she didn't make me change my opinion of you with her visit, and you haven't succeeded completely. That can only happen if you keep proving yourself to her. Tell her we're just drawing a veil."

"I will. I'm ashamed Beth felt she had to apologise for me."

"Of course she did," Chris said. "She loves you. Surely you expected her to stand up for you?"

Matthew looked chastened. "I didn't take it for granted this time," he said. "I'm learning."

"We'll make an appointment with the solicitors and get things moving, now your conscience allows us to," Geoff said.

Matthew looked at him with respect. It was good to be

answerable to a man like Geoff who spoke his mind. He respected his integrity and resolve. He'd not behaved well and understood the way Geoff was reserving the right to alter his opinion. Anyone who looked out for Beth was high in his estimation. "Thank you," he said.

It was a relief to Matthew that everything was sorted. He was reconciled to living at the Willows with his family. Not so long ago, he thought, I was living alone in the cavernous old vicarage in the very same village, and that never bothered my conscience. He smiled to himself. Now *that* would make a wonderful women's refuge.

He was his old self as he entered the cottage. He had a kiss and a hug for Beth and a cuddle for Gwynnie. "I've been to see your parents," he said. "I've apologised for behaving like an idiot."

"How did it go?"

"Quite well, I think. Your dad made it clear he's reserving judgment about me, but he accepted my apology. They're going to see their solicitor to get things moving. Your mum was lovely."

He watched Beth's face break into a beaming smile and felt relieved they could move past the whole affair. "I didn't ask how long it will all take."

"There's no hurry, as long as we end up there." She took Gwynnie from his arms so he could go to take a shower. "Diana called this afternoon. Janos's case comes to trial at the end of next month. The word is he's going to plead guilty to try for a lighter sentence. He's realised, apparently, the police have enough proof to put him away for a long time."

"That's good," he said. "It will make it easier on Edward and Alison in court. I'll be glad when he's sentenced, and we can all move on."

"Edward, Diana and Alison will move on, but they'll never

get over it completely. Neither will Gemma."

"Remind me to always take your advice," he said, referring to his error over The Willows as much as the Janos case. "You're a very wise wife."

He meant it. As he took his shower, he reflected on how skilfully her thoughtful reasoning led her to the correct conclusions time after time. He could not believe he'd jeopardised her trust so wantonly.

I won't be taking you for granted again. Ever.

Matthew and his family discussed their forthcoming news about moving to The Willows over dinner.

"We'll have plenty of room for you," Beth said to Josie. "You can have a whole floor to yourself and still be part of our family. It will be marvellous."

Matthew saw uncertainty cross Josie's face. "What's wrong?"

"I've realised it's a big thing for you to let me move in permanently. It might be better if I found myself a flat," she said. "I don't think I should be imposing myself on you permanently."

He scrutinised her face but could not discern if that was what she wanted or if that was what she thought they wanted. He laid his hand on her arm. "You can have a home with us for as long as you want it," he said. "You once heard me ask when you were going back there, but I didn't mean it. I was angry about other things. With Janos. Truly, Josie, you have a home with us if you want it."

"I know you mean it now, but I'll get old and needy. I don't want to become a burden."

"You're family. Family is never a burden."

"Bless you. You're a good man," Josie said, "and a clever one, though you don't always act like it." She had never lost her teasing tone with him. "There's nothing I'd like better than to live with you all. I feel alive with you, able to cope without Sidney.""

He agreed with Josie's assessment of him. He didn't always act like a good and intelligent man. He would, he decided, have to do better.

CHAPTER ELEVEN

The weeks leading up to Janos' trial saw the legal agreements about The Willows finalised. Beth's parents packed up and went on their way to Australia, and she started their preparations to move in.

Matthew's sister, Bronwen, had flown over from New Zealand to Wales to assess their parents' needs. She told him she wasn't happy he hadn't managed to visit them, and said she had had to take control. He knew she was right to be angry.

In the first week she concluded her father wasn't coping and her mother needed specialist care. She had set about finding a residential home for them and lined up a few to visit. She asked Matthew to go along with her to find the most suitable one, so he hastily arranged a trip to Llanelli.

He was horrified when he saw the change in his parents. It had been rapid and dramatic. His mother didn't recognise him and mistook him for her long-dead brother. She called him Huw throughout the visit. His father had lost weight, his clothes were hanging off him. He was struggling with his balance and was shuffling rather than walking. He had lost his familiar upright posture. Matthew was shocked by his curved spine and lowered head.

He talked with his sister late into the night. Bron was analytical and clear. She was positive that both should move into a home, arguing they would be together, well-fed and properly looked after. Matthew hated the idea of either of them being moved into a home, especially his independent-minded father. He could accept his mother was beyond knowing where she was and urgently needed help, but he was convinced his proud, self-sufficient father would deteriorate in such a place.

"He's not self-sufficient anymore, Matt," she said. "It's as if he's lost his self-respect too since Mam got worse. I've sorted things out since I got here. They were both pretty smelly when I arrived. Neither of them can manage the bath now. To be honest, they need more than the Church Care Team can provide."

Matthew shook his head with disbelief. He sighed, guilt descending on him like a lead weight. "Dad said things were fine every time I called. and what with getting ready for the move and everything, I just left everything to you. I've not even been over. I should have."

"Yes, you should." His sister did not hold back. "It's all very well saving the world, but your own parents were struggling."

He nodded, knowing she was correct. "If we find a place for Mam, maybe Dad could come and live with us."

She looked at him in contempt. "And pigs might fly," she said. "Dad wouldn't move to the Midlands and leave Mam on her own. You must know that." She softened her tone. "The truth is, I've got to go back to my lot pretty soon and you're fully stretched. We have no choice. We have to find them somewhere they can be looked after. Neither of us can take that on."

"What about the house? I know Mam won't care one way or the other, but Dad loves this place."

"Bricks and mortar, Matt. That's what it boils down to. We can't make it into a shrine and pretend they're coming back one day. The fees are going to be expensive, particularly for Mam. They'll need every penny."

"Bron, they're our parents. We owe them." He could see the sadness in her face as she constructed her reply.

"Let's be honest. I'm not a hypocrite, Matt. I've hardly prioritised them, have I? It's eighteen years since I moved to New Zealand, and I've not given them much thought. You've made the odd trip here since you went to university, but not much more, and you were the only one in visiting distance."

He nodded. What she had said was true. He and Bron had got on with their own lives for years, and it was no use pretending otherwise.

"Before you dash off to confessions," she said, "they've got on with their lives too. Up until now they've been fit and well. They've been here, there, and everywhere since Dad retired. I've lost count of the cruises they've done. They haven't been pining for us."

He looked at his sister and marvelled at how clearly she assessed the situation. Every word she spoke was true. There was no honour in taking on responsibility at this late hour when he'd felt no obligation up until then. She could remove emotion from her decision making and be totally objective. He was crippled with regrets and the desire to solve everything single-handed.

"We don't go to confessions," he muttered, unable to reply adequately to the blistering truth she was trying to make him face.

"I know that, fat-head." She laughed. "I was joking. Look, Matt, you're my brother and I love you. I've not visited you in all those years and you've not been over to see me. If I dropped dead tonight, I wouldn't want you to be consumed with guilt because you thought you'd neglected me. That's how I feel about Mam and Dad."

"Bron." He sighed deeply. "My mind's all over the place. You're my very wise older sister and I need to think over what you've said."

"You certainly do. You've always had a saviour complex, trying to make everything better. Little brother, it's time to learn you can solve some problems without taking them directly on to your own shoulders." She drained her glass then dropped a kiss on his forehead. "Try to get some sleep. Staying awake worrying won't make things any better."

The visits to the nursing homes proved harrowing for Matthew, even though he had been used to visiting the ones in his old parish. God's waiting room, he thought as he surveyed the residents, dozing in their chairs in the day rooms. He hated the thought that his parents were going to join them. He was sure his dad would disappear into oblivion in a stagnant place like that.

The last one offered hope. The upper floor offered specialised care for dementia and Alzheimer patients. He liked the vibrant surroundings and the respectful way the staff treated the residents.

The lower floor was set up for people like his father. Some of the residents were dozing in their chairs, but others were reading or doing crossword puzzles. Two elderly gentlemen were playing chess in a corner and a group of women were working on a jigsaw on a large table at the side of the room. He felt himself breathe a little easier. Here was a place where the elderly lived rather than faded away. It was a busy room, and unlike the other places, it was not dominated by a huge television that no one was watching.

The manager said she would be able to accommodate their parents in a double room whilst ever their mother's condition made that possible. It seemed the most suitable solution to a heart-breaking situation.

As they drove back, Bron once again demonstrated her confidence in her ability to resolve everything. "I'll take Dad to visit there this afternoon," she said. "You can stay with Mam. He'll see it's what's best for her, and once he does, I know he'll want to be there with her. We'll take things from there."

"I'm not convinced he'll agree," Matthew said.

"That's because you'd give him the choice when there really is none. They both need looking after. It's up to me to make him see that."

He sighed. "I'm the one who does this sort of thing for a living, and when it comes to my own parents I'm floundering."

"That's because you're awash with guilt," she said. "It's not helping. Our dad is covered in bites and bruises from when Mam turns nasty. He can't cope and he'd he useless on his own. He can't drive now, and he's so unsteady on his feet, he can't use the bus. He wouldn't be able to visit her, and that would kill him."

He lapsed into silence, aware of the truths his sister had spoken yet still feeling raw at the impending changes they were going to make to their parents' lives.

"Matt, I can do this," Bron said, breaking the silence. "You should go home to Beth and your baby tomorrow."

"I can't leave. That's not fair on you, Bron."

"It's easier for me that way. Olwen Jones will help. We've never lost touch, and she's been popping round every day. We'll give notice on the house, pack up the treasures Mam and Dad will need, sort the rest out and then get a dealer in to clear the place. I'll sell the car when I'm ready to go home. I'll need it till then."

Matthew looked at his sister in amazement. "That's so clinical," he said.

"That's how I'll cope. If I get sentimental, I'll cave in. I have to leave them when it's all sorted, and I'll need peace of mind to do that. If we try to do it together on your weekend visits it will just drag on and I'll run out of time."

"We'll see how you get on with Dad this afternoon," he said, "and then we'll decide."

"Okay, but you already know what I think."

Matthew sat watching television with his mother whilst Bron took their father to visit the home. He could see she was restless.

"Where's Arwyn?" she asked.

"Bron's taken him for a drive," he replied. "They won't be long."

She was quiet for two minutes before asking where Arwyn was.

Matthew gave the same reply, making his tone as reassuring as he could. A pattern had been set. Every couple of minutes she asked where Arwyn was.

"I'll make us a nice cup of tea," Matthew said, trying to break the pattern. "We could have some biscuits too."

He went into the kitchen with a heavy heart, seeing firsthand the dependence his formerly capable mother had developed on her husband. He was waiting for the kettle to boil when he heard her opening the pantry door.

"What are you doing, Mam?"

"Getting my coat," she said, taking it down from the back of the door.

"I'm making a pot of tea," he said. "We're not going out this afternoon."

"I'm meeting Arwyn at the Nelli. We're going to the pictures." She was putting her arms into the sleeves.

The Theatr Nelli, the Odeon Cinema, was the magnificent art deco building in the town centre where she and Arwyn had done their courting. Time had no meaning for her now. Her past was her present, as real as anything in her life.

"No, Mam," he said. "Not today." He went to ease her coat from her shoulders, but as he tried to, she let loose a string of abuse at him that took him completely by surprise. He had never heard her swear, and he had no idea she was fluent in obscenities.

He managed to get her coat off her arms, but as soon as they were free, she pummelled him with all her might, insisting she was going *to the pictures.*

Matthew was at a loss. Her strength surprised him as she pounded away. It was against every instinct to use any degree of force in restraining her, so he circled her in his arms in what he hoped was a compassionate hold. He spoke softly to her, telling her how much he loved her and that everything would be all right. She writhed and struggled but he held fast, his voice remaining soothing and reassuring.

Eventually the aggression faded, and she quietened in his arms. Relief swept through him. "Come on, Mam. Let's get you in the other room and then we'll have that cup of tea."

"Where's Arwyn?" she asked, as if nothing had happened.

"Bron's taken him for a drive," he answered.

Later that evening, when Bron had taken their mother upstairs to wash her hair, Matthew and his father had a chance to talk. It was the first time they had been alone together since he arrived.

"What did you think of the place?" he asked. The subject had not been raised whilst his mother had been present.

His father looked directly at him. "It's exactly what your mother needs," he said. "It's sad, Matthew, but we have to face facts, boy. I can't look after her anymore. She's gone downhill so fast it's hard to believe." He rolled up his sleeve to show his son the bites and bruises on his arms. They were worse than Matthew had expected. "Terrible, it is, terrible."

"And what about you, Dad?"

"Where your mother goes, I go. For better or worse, I vowed, and I meant it, boy. But I've told them straight I can't share her room. They said we could be together, but I told them no." He shook his head in sorrow. "She takes it into her head, see, she's going out in the middle of the night. That's when she gets nasty. Terrible it is. I can't always hold on to her." He pulled out his handkerchief and wiped his eyes.

Matthew had never seen his father cry and they sat in

silence until he composed himself. "They have movement sensors in the rooms, Dad. They'll know when she gets out of bed, and someone will go in to keep her safe. They're used to it. They'll know what to do."

His father nodded. "Such a beautiful woman, boy, and now she has no shame. Her language . . . she swears like a fishwife, she does. I don't know what to do with her, boy. We need help, so don't you go feeling guilty. This is beyond you and your sister. Your sister knows only too well. She's lived with it since she's come home."

"But the house, Dad. You'll have to give up your home."

"Home? Home, you say? This stopped being a home when we went to New Zealand and your mother started to go downhill. It's a prison now, boy. A bloody prison. That's what it is. I can't leave her for a minute. She follows me round, and I can't take her out because I'm so doddery."

"Why did you keep telling me everything was fine, Dad? I'd have come over straight away. I wouldn't have known if Bron hadn't come over."

"I didn't tell you because I'm her husband and I should be the one to take care of her. For better or worse. Do you think I want you and your sister seeing your mother like this? Pride we have, boy. Pride."

Renewed respect for his father surged through him. He saw again his father was forged of steel. The last of generations of miners, Arwyn Thomas had left the pits in November 1986 when Carway Fawr closed for the last time. Finding work had not been easy and he and his wife had to keep their young family fed and clothed. There had been times when their pride was all that kept them going as they struggled to put food on the table.

Maybe, Matthew reflected, this had been where his passion for helping the underprivileged and his distaste for the trappings of wealth had come from. Strange, he reflected, similar circumstances had made Janos turn to crime. He pushed those thoughts out of his head. It was no time to psycho-analyse that man.

He knew his parents had shielded him and his sister from the worst of the poverty. They had always been clean and fed and had thought little of it at the time. It had been his parents who had struggled, not him and Bron, and he loved them for it.

His father had been one of the fortunate ones. A skilled engineer, he had eventually managed to find decent work at British Steel and finally got his family back on a steady financial keel.

His father's voice brought him back from those memories. "That place is beautiful, boy, beautiful. It's like a palace. So don't you worry any more. Your mam will be grand there, and so will I. I'll see her every day." He wiped his eyes again. "The truth is, boy, she needs to be safe and well-looked after, and I'm ashamed to say I can't do that anymore. I can't even look after myself properly."

There were tears in Matthew's eyes, too. He had never hugged his father for years. Hugs had been left behind along with his boyhood. That evening, he put his arms round his father and held him tight. They shed tears together.

"There's lovely," Bron said, smiling, and feigning the Welsh lilt she had lost years before when she saw them. "Now you know you can go back to Beth and Gwynnie with a clear conscience. Dad and I will sort everything out."

"You go home, boy," his father said," but bring that baby girl to see me as soon as you can."

Matthew wiped his sleeve across his eyes. "I love you all so much," he said.

"Soft in the head, you are," Bron said, wiping a tear away too. "Soft in the head."

Matthew had plenty to think about as he drove home. He could accept the inevitability of his mother's transfer to a care home — even the doctors were astonished at the speed of her decline. He felt guilty for not realising what his father had been going through. It had been a shock to see the diminished man his father had become, and he was still struggling to accept it.

His mind turned to Janos once again. Gemma had told him about where that man's ruthlessness had stemmed from. He had known hardship as he was growing up, and it had made him bitter and resentful, determined to climb out of poverty and tread relentlessly over those who were well off. Poverty had crushed Janos' father, leaving his son with no example to follow. It made him appreciate his own father even more.

He was glad to see Beth and Gwynnie. Their house was cluttered with packing cases and stripped bare of the belongings that had made it seem like home, but they were waiting for him at the door, summoned by the sound of his car.

There was much catching up to do. Beth wanted to hear the news from Llanelli. It made him feel better to talk to her about the situation he'd found in Wales, because he could be totally honest with her. He could see the care and concern etching itself on to her face as she listened. He knew she understood his pain.

Changing the subject, he asked how the plans for the move were coming along. She had a small van booked to transfer their belongings over to The Willows the next day. Everything was ready there. The beds were made and Gwynnie's new toddler furniture had been delivered and assembled. He could hear the excitement in Beth's voice as she told him how she and Josie had moved the essentials over in readiness.

Josie came in at that point.

"Are you all packed?" he asked.

"Yes. We moved my stuff over this morning and cleared the rest. The van man gave me grief over all those stairs at The Willows," she said. "I told him I'm twice his age and I wasn't moaning."

"And you're sure you've made the right decision?"

"It's a bit late to be asking me that." She laughed. "I've sent the rest of my stuff to the auction, and I took the keys back to the council this afternoon."

Matthew laughed too. "It's good to be back with you all. I've missed you all."

"We've missed you too," Beth said.

"I've not," Josie said. The banter between her and Matthew had long been part of their relationship. "No mess to clear up."

He looked round at the chaotic stacks of packing cases and raised his eyebrows. "So I see," he said.

She flapped at him with the tea towel she was holding, just as she used to do with her duster in the old days at The Manor. "And I suppose you won't be around when we unpack this lot."

"That's right," he said, feeling grateful that his home was the loving, happy place he'd always been used to.

CHAPTER TWELVE

M atthew had no wish to attend Janos' sentencing, but Al-ison, Edward and Diana wanted him there. They said they needed his support to face the man who had brought havoc to their lives. He took his place alongside them in the public gallery of the Crown Court, noting Brooksie was there too, holding Alison's hand.

Janos had pleaded guilty from the start. The evidence against him was overwhelming and the police told Matthew a custodial sentence was inevitable. They said he'd accepted his only hope of reducing his term in jail was by admitting the offences of attempted murder and extortion.

Edward and Alison were relieved not to have to give evidence, but both wanted closure. They needed to see this man punished for all the damage he had done. Diana understood he wouldn't be facing charges for what had happened to Gemma, but she said she wanted to look him in the eye as he was sentenced.

Matthew could see the nervous anxiety in his friends. They were speaking too quickly as they chatted before the hearing started, and he could see they were all breathing rapidly. He felt for each one of them, wanted to be there for them, but was silently wishing he wasn't.

He had his own demons. They were the demons that always tormented him when he found forgiveness a challenge. Janos' treatment of Gemma seemed to him as bad as Wayne Jackson's treatment of Beth. It had awoken all the old anger and desire for revenge.

He understood these were the same demons that had driven Janos to try to take Alison's life that night. The man had become obsessed with the need for revenge. It did not sit well with his conscience that he wanted Janos to suffer.

He sighed at the parallels he saw. They had both known poverty and both had been shaped by their fathers' responses to it. They had followed different paths. What scared him was the realisation they both had a common taste for revenge. He prayed the sentence that day would bring would prove sufficient for him to let his need for retribution go.

His thoughts crystalised as he saw Janos' face as he took his place in the dock. It seemed contorted with hatred and fury. He knew then he was looking at a man with no conscience, no regrets, and that knowledge quietened his troubled soul. He was not like Janos.

The proceedings did not take long. The judge sentenced Janos to twenty years' imprisonment. In his summing up, he denounced him as an evil individual who had wrought pain and suffering on the lives of too many people.

Matthew knew the sneer of contempt on Janos' face as the judge addressed him directly was no act of bravado. He also detected fear in his eyes as sentence was pronounced. He would be under no illusions of what lay ahead. Months on remand would have taught him that.

Matthew took his friends to a nearby pub afterwards. He noted there was no sense of triumph within the group, just relief that Janos had been given a long sentence and was out of their lives.

"Thank God that's over," said Edward, drawing heavily on his pint of beer.

"It will never be over for Gemma," Diana said. "She's nineteen years old and that man has ruined her life forever. He's the reason she's left us."

"She might come back to us when she hears what's happened today," Edward said, trying to console her.

Diana's eyes flashed. "She was going to university. Now she's making ends meet working in a hotel, too ashamed of what she's done to face us. He can rot in hell as far as I'm concerned."

Silence fell on the group. Matthew had never heard Diana speak out like that before, and as he thought about what she'd said, he couldn't blame her.

"I'd have liked to see the blighter hanged after what he tried to do to Alison," Brooksie said.

"I'll drink to that," Alison said suddenly, breaking her silence. She raised her glass and chinked it against his. "I've never been one to forgive and forget." She looked directly at Matthew. "And I sincerely hope you won't be visiting him in prison to minister unto him."

Matthew raised both his hands, palms towards Alison. "I couldn't bear to be in the same room as him," he said. He tried to lighten the tone. "What is that I see glistening on your ring finger? You kept quiet about that little trinket."

Alison stretched her hand out to allow them to see the solitaire.

"Wow!" Diana said. "That's a beauty. Congratulations to both of you."

"It was my grandmother's," Brooksie said. "Alison is the first woman to wear it since I inherited it."

Matthew could see the joy in his face as he spoke.

"He means he didn't let his previous wives get their hands on it," Alison chuckled. "I'm the lucky one."

"*He's* the lucky one," corrected Matthew, raising his glass. "Congratulations."

It was a relief to them all to have something positive to talk about, and the stress around the table seeped away as Alison and Brooksie's excitement emerged.

'So, how's life in The Willows, Matthew? Or should I call

you sir now?" Alison asked.

He could see her eyes dancing with mischief. "Beth's made it feel like home already," he said. "When we sit round the kitchen table together, it's amazing."

"Can't bring yourself to use the dining room yet, then?" Alison teased.

"We will when you all come round to dinner." He smiled at her. "Beth will want to celebrate your engagement. I think we all need to do something positive after all this."

"Agreed," Edward said.

"I'll bring dessert," Diana said.

"I'll bring champagne," Brooksie said.

"And I'll bring my sophisticated repartee and my diamond," Alison laughed. "I'm going up in the world, so I have to cultivate some airs and graces."

"Then our dinner may have to be delayed for quite some time," Matthew replied, winking across at her.

"Touché, Saint Matthew, touché."

Matthew welcomed the calm that descended on them all once Janos was safely locked away.

Alison and Brooksie were working with him, supporting the new centre in Derby, and bringing influential supporters onboard. They were also working on the refurbishment of Brooksley Hall, wanting a quick completion of the renovations to recoup some of the outlay. He noted Alison was applying her business brain and had reined in her extravagant tastes.

He was glad Gemma was in weekly contact with her parents. Whilst she was still refusing all requests to visit home, she was keeping in touch.

He was pleased Josie had settled immediately in the flat on the top floor of The Willows. She was minding Gwynnie a couple of mornings whilst Beth concentrated on her accountancy commissions.

Matthew was seeing the first centre start to fulfil its potential and was ploughing ahead with the one in Derby. He had adjusted quickly to living at The Willows and was enjoying seeing Beth's contentment there. She had even started attending the family services at the village church with him and Gwynnie, whose baptism was booked.

This all proved extremely satisfying for Matthew, thankful at last for a period when his brain was not feverishly troubled by anxieties. His respite did not last for long, however.

He went home after a particularly long day at work to find Gemma seated at the kitchen table.

"Gemma's brought her baby to see us," Beth said. She nodded towards the baby seat he had failed to notice. A crop of very dark hair was peeping out of the blanket covering the sleeping child.

He sat down with a bump, shocked beyond belief.

"Did you know?" he asked Beth.

"Of course not."

Gwynnie was at his side, desperate to sit on his knee. "Daddy, new baby," she said.

He lifted her on to his lap.

"Gemma has a long story to tell. She's staying for dinner, and she's going to tell us all about it when Gwynnie's in bed."

"Have you been home?" he asked, thinking of Edward and Diana.

Gemma shook her head.

"Do your parents know?"

She shook her head again.

"Gemma!" There was exasperation in his voice.

"It's complicated," she said.

"Having babies usually is," he replied, frowning at her. "Your parents deserve to hear your story before anyone else does. You're compromising our friendship by coming here first and involving us." He knew how much her parents had suffered since she had got herself involved with Janos, and how much more they'd suffered since she walked away. He had no wish to add to that.

"I always come here first. You and Beth give me the courage to face them."

"Then we'll face them together. They can come here tonight, and we'll all hear what you have to say."

"It's taken Gemma a lot of courage to come here," Beth said, tears in her eyes.

"True," he agreed, "but that doesn't mean we have to deceive her parents. I mean it, Gemma. Beth and I will always support you, you know that, but always alongside your parents. As I said, we'll face them together. You know you'll have to face them sooner or later."

Gemma looked at him, and he could see she was silently begging him not to involve them.

"I'm going for a shower," he said, planting a kiss on Gwynnie's head and putting her down on the floor. "Talk to Beth, Gemma. She'll help you to see this is the only way forward. Your mum and dad mustn't get to know after us. They don't deserve that."

"I know." Her voice sounded wretched. "I'll call them."

"Why was he being like that?" Gemma asked as soon as he'd gone upstairs.

"He's spent hours with your dad and knows how much he's hurting," Beth said. "What happened to you nearly broke him, and Matthew was the only person he could confide in."

"Dad always seemed fine when I phoned," Gemma said.

"Your mum and dad have both been putting on brave faces. Your mum's been round here a lot. She's not doing so well either." Beth said. "Your calls are all that's kept them going."

"I had a lot to deal with," Gemma said.

"I can see that," Beth replied, inclining her head towards the baby, who was just beginning to stir and whimper.

Gemma scrabbled about in her bag and pulled out the baby's bottle. "Could you feed him?" she asked, holding it out towards Beth.

Beth looked hard at Gemma's face, trying to detect clues about why she wanted her to feed him. She could find none. "I'll put the kettle on," she said. "Will he want changing?"

"Don't bother with the kettle, I give it to him cold. He's used to it like that. I suppose he'll want a clean nappy." She sighed and searched through the bag again in a distracted way.

Beth was growing concerned. Could Gemma not be bothered to warm his bottles? She didn't seem interested in him at all. She moved the blanket aside and unfastened the straps before lifting the baby from his chair.

"Give me the nappy," Beth said. "I'll change him. We'll go up to Gwynnie's room. Do you want to come?"

Gemma shook her head. "I'll stay with Gwynnie down here. I'll phone my parents."

Beth snuggled the baby to her and felt his soft dark hair against her cheek. She breathed in deeply, expecting a sweet baby aroma to fill her nostrils. She was disappointed. The smell from the baby wasn't offensive, but it wasn't fresh. She dropped a kiss on his tiny head and took him upstairs.

When she'd changed him, she took him into her bedroom where Matthew was dressing after his shower.

"It didn't take you long to get your hands on him," he said with a smile. "What's his name?"

"He doesn't have one. Gemma's not registered his birth yet," she raised her eyebrows at her husband to try to convey her concern.

"Oh," he said, clearly detecting her signal.

"Try not to be so harsh with her," Beth said. "It's great

you're getting Edward and Diana round, but Gemma's been through an awful lot all on her own."

He nodded. "Point taken," he said.

"She's very young to be facing all this," Beth said. She looked at the baby tenderly, stroking his soft dark skin. "He's clearly not Janos' child. You can't inherit a fake tan."

"It means his father was one of the rapists. I don't know if that makes it better or worse."

"Neither do I," she said. "But I do know that Gemma's struggling with it all and needs a lot of support."

Matthew nodded. "The sooner we get Edward and Diana involved, the better for all of them."

"Gemma's calling them now."

"Good." He took the baby from Beth and held him close. "Poor little soul," he said.

Beth looked at Matthew's face. It was full of love and compassion, and she saw tears welling in his eyes. She knew, despite the harsh way he'd spoken to Gemma, he was as concerned as she was.

Edward and Diana arrived quickly. They were flustered, clearly keen to see Gemma but also obviously unprepared for the shock that faced them. Gemma had insisted she must face them with the news herself.

She opened the door and was engulfed in their embraces as soon as they stepped in. They were all in tears.

"Before you go in there," she said, nodding towards the room they were about to enter, "I have something to tell you. It's going to come as a shock."

She saw the anxious look on their faces and took a deep breath. "I had a baby last week. He's in there, waiting to meet you. I'll understand if you want to turn round and go home."

Diana grabbed Edward's arm and Gemma watched his face turn grey. She thought he was going to pass out.

"Dad," she said. "Say something." She watched him shake his head as if he were trying to clear his thoughts.

"Take us in there," he said after a pause. "We'd better meet him."

Gemma breathed out heavily. That was more encouraging than she had dared to hope. She opened the door and led them into the sitting room, where Beth was holding the baby.

Diana extended her arms and Beth rose and passed the child to her. She pulled him gently towards her and sat down.

"I'm going to get us all a drink whilst you take this in," Beth said. "You both look as if you need a cup of tea. Matthew, can you help?" They both left the room.

When they returned, Edward was holding the baby and Diana was by his side, her index finger stroking his tiny hand. Gemma was sitting on the other side of the room, turning her bracelet round and round. She was getting ready to tell her story, and she was summoning up all her courage to be able to begin.

"Before you start, Gem," Diana said, "you need to know we're here for you. We can see what's happened and we'll work it out. You don't need to be scared."

"I'm not scared, Mum. I'm ashamed. So ashamed that I ran away to keep all this from you."

"You didn't need to do that," Diana said. "We love you no matter what."

"It's all my fault," Gemma said and took a deep breath. "When Mum took me to the clinic, they gave me the morning after pill. I kept on being sick so the next day I took the second one, just like they said. I was still being sick that day too, but it was happening every time I thought of those videos. They were enough to make me vomit."

"I remember. You couldn't keep anything down," Diana said.

Gemma nodded. "I'd been on the pill for a while, I'd taken two morning-after pills, and I thought it would be fine. I'd done what they'd told me at the clinic. I honestly thought I'd been responsible."

"When did you find out?" her mother asked.

"The day I left home. The day I came to see Beth and she made me tell you I was leaving. I'd done five pregnancy tests by then and they were all positive. It had been hard enough facing you after what I'd done, I couldn't let you know the mess I was in."

She saw the panic in her mother's eyes. "Did you tell Beth?" she asked. She turned to Beth. "Did you know all along?"

"No," Beth said. "Absolutely not."

"If it hadn't been for Beth I'd have disappeared completely. I was so ashamed," she said.

"Didn't you think of getting rid of it?" Edward spoke for the first time.

"Of course I did, but I couldn't do it. Bottom line," she said, "I didn't want it, but I couldn't have a termination. Its father was a filthy rapist, but its mother didn't have to end its life before it started." She drew her knees up to her chest, just as she'd done in the old days at the cottage. She hugged them and rocked gently.

"That's a bit extreme, Gem," her mother said.

"It's how I felt back then. I was a mess." She was trying to find the words to continue her story.

"Where did you go? How did you manage?" Diana asked.

Those questions were easy to answer. "I drove down to Warwick. I've no idea why, apart from liking it when we'd been on university open days. I stayed in a B and B until I got a job at a fancy hotel and restaurant. It came with accommodation, so I just about made ends meet. I'd got a bit of money from when I worked . . ." She paused. She was going to say *when I worked for Janos,* but the words stuck in her throat, " . . . from when I worked in the office to get the baby stuff."

"Did you look after yourself? Did you eat properly?" Diana

asked.

"I tried my best. I signed on at a medical centre and I went to all my ante-natal appointments and scans. I took my iron pills and my folic acid. I didn't drink. I did everything by the book."

"Were you able to keep on working?"

"Yes. I was well and I didn't get very big. It took months for the people at work to realise I was pregnant. I went two weeks over my due date, so they admitted me into hospital in the end and induced me."

"Were you all on your own?" Diana asked, her voice breaking.

"Yes, and I deserved to be after everything I'd done," she said. "My fault. My mess."

Diana made as if to go over to her. She still had the baby in her arms.

"Don't, Mum, just don't," Gemma said, as if the potential approach of the child unnerved her.

"So, what have you called him?" Edward asked.

"I haven't given him a name."

"Can't make your mind up?" he asked.

Diana spoke quickly. "You've not bonded, have you Gem?"

Gemma shook her head. "I'm a dreadful person. I can't bear to look at him. I don't know who his father is, I don't even know his name. I know by the colour of his skin it isn't Janos, but, beyond that, I haven't a clue. Just looking at him makes me feel nauseous because it makes me think of that video."

She saw a heavy mood descend on everyone. She sensed they understood but had no idea what to say. "I'm going to have him adopted," she said. "I want to forget all this ever happened, and I want to get my life back on track."

"Gem!" Diana gasped. She moved the baby closer to her breast and dropped a kiss on his head.

"Don't, Mum," she said once again. She had thought this through so often she knew exactly how her mother would react as soon as she held the baby. "I want you all to listen. I'd like Matthew and Beth to adopt the baby." She saw them look at each other and recognised the shock on their faces. Her mother looked distraught.

"Hear me out. I don't have any right to ask any of this, I know that, but this is what I'd like. I'd like my parents back. I want to go home and be close to you, like we used to be. If you take in the baby, I can't do that. I couldn't bear to see you fussing over him. I really need my mum and dad for myself right now."

She looked round and saw shock registered on everyone's face. "As I said, I've no right to ask any of this, but this is me being honest. If Beth and Matthew adopt the baby, I know he'll be loved. I need to know he's well looked after. I know they'd let you be proper grandparents, whereas that won't happen if strangers adopt him. I want to keep the door open. One day, I might be able to have some kind of relationship with him. Beth and Matthew might let me into his life if I sort myself out. I want to go to Warwick in September and take up that course and get myself back to where I once was. That's what I'd like. I'll understand if you all tell me to take him, get back in the car and clear off."

Gemma was unnerved by the silence in the room. It made her want to keep talking to fill in the void, but she knew she had nothing more worth saying. The silence went on and on.

Eventually Matthew spoke. "We can't make life-changing decisions like this right now," he said, and everyone nodded. "There are laws, Gemma. We can't just adopt him because you've chosen us. There are procedures."

"I know," Gemma said, "But I can't spend one more hour with that baby." She spoke from the bottom of her heart. "I'd never hurt him, but just looking at him makes me feel sick. What his father—whichever one it is—did to me isn't his fault, but I can't stop thinking about it and it's driving me crazy. I could block it out whilst I was pregnant, but now I have to look after him."

Silence descended once again.

"Here's a suggestion," Matthew said. "It's only a suggestion, and someone might have a better idea. Gemma, you need some space, and you need to be with your parents right now." Gemma nodded. "Your baby could stay here with Beth and me this weekend. You three can spend the time talking and deciding what you really want to do. Beth and I can discuss adoption. Just think that over before you speak."

Gemma was looking at him in gratitude. "That would be perfect, but I do know I've no right to ask anything off any of you."

"I just want to spend time with my girl. Edward, what about you? What do you think?" Diana asked. Gemma could see her mother was desperate for her dad to speak up.

"I need time to get my head round this and the chance to talk with you on our own. You've dropped a bombshell, Gem. I need some time with your mum."

Gemma nodded.

"We can look after him," Beth said. "We've got all Gwynnie's baby gear."

"Then let's do it, and all bear in mind that no other decisions were made here tonight. This is no time for snap decisions. This little man's future is at stake," Matthew said.

Edward stood up and offered his hand to Matthew.

Gemma watched them shake hands and then hug each other. She finally understood what Beth had meant when she said her father had suffered and had turned to Matthew for support.

Diana handed the baby to Beth. Gemma saw the regret in her eyes as she let him go and realised how much her mother wanted to be part of the child's life. She sniffed away her tears and spoke to them all.

"Thank you. I can sleep in my own bed tonight and know he's taken care of. It's the first glimmer of hope I've had in months."

* * * *

Beth settled the baby into his carry cot at the side of their bed after she had given changed him and given him his late feed. Matthew was sitting up, reading. He closed his book and put it down.

"You're getting attached," he said. "I'm not sure that's a good thing."

"I'm okay," she said. "I know we're in a minefield. I'm making myself be sensible."

"Theoretically, could you adopt him?"

She sighed. "We've never considered adopting. We both love Gwynnie so much it worries me that we could never feel the same about someone else's child."

He nodded. "I know exactly what you mean," he said. "I'm all mixed up. I couldn't give my parents the care they need, and yet now I'm thinking about taking in someone else's child. I feel like a hypocrite."

Beth snuggled closer to him. "We couldn't give your mum the specialist care she needs, and your dad wouldn't leave her. There was no choice. There's a choice here."

"Maybe it's easier for you to be objective," he said.

"You'll know better how you feel after you've slept on it. "

"Perhaps," he said. "We have so much space here . . . it could work."

"And maybe there's a plan for him after all. We just need to be sure what it is." Beth sighed. "Maybe this little man is part of the future for us here at The Willows."

"Beth, you mustn't let yourself get attached. He's here for the weekend. Everything beyond that is too uncertain."

"But you're not against the idea?"

"Not against it, no. But far from certain about it either."

"I'm holding on to the fact I loved Martha and Harry, and I looked after them, but I was able to let them go."

Matthew put his arms around her and hugged her. "You chose me instead," he said.

"And now I've got you and Gwynnie. No one comes before you two. But, if we took this little one on, he'd have to be loved just as much."

"The question we have to answer, if it comes to that, is can we do that?"

"We know his father is not a good man, whoever he is. We can't dispute that. Could we compensate for what the gene pool has donated?" Beth asked.

"Nature versus nurture," Matthew said. "Who knows? But someone's going to have to try. We'll have to talk about it tomorrow. We both need time to process this. I guess it will be all we think about."

Beth did not sleep well that night, and she knew by his sighing and ceaseless movement that Matthew didn't either. The baby's cries for his next feed found both still wide awake.

She looked at Matthew as she sat feeding the child. "We have to do this," she said. "I can't let him go to strangers."

"Neither can I," he said. "But you do realise it will take time, and Gemma could change her mind?"

She nodded. "We've got to say yes."

They heard nothing from the Hoopers over that weekend but expected them to arrive after seven on Sunday evening. By that time they hoped to have Gwynnie bathed and in bed.

Matthew watched the baby whilst Beth bathed Gwynnie and put her to bed.

"Well, little man, you smell a lot sweeter than you did when you arrived," he said, picking him up and inhaling the freshly bathed scent from the fluffy thatch of dark hair.

"Whatever shall we do with you?" he asked. "Maybe we'll find out tonight. Beth and I have decided we'd like you to be our very own little boy. You don't know this, little man, but I've been saying a lot of prayers for you. I'm hoping The Boss will get us to the right answer, because the rest of your life is at stake."

He still had the boy in his arms when the doorbell rang. He let the Hoopers in and led them to the sitting room, passing the baby to Diana. He could see the love in her eyes as she looked at the little child.

"Beth won't be long," he said. "She's just settling Gwynnie."

"How are your parents doing?" Edward asked.

"Better than I'd dared hope. My dad was saying he's found someone to talk politics with for hours on end, apparently. Fortunately, they're in agreement, so they put the world to rights as they talk. He says my mum thinks she's on holiday in a hotel with her girlfriends."

"I'm glad it's working out. Such a worry for you," Edward said. "You could do without all this. I know you were hoping to get over there this weekend. You must be fed up with us."

Matthew looked him directly in the eyes. "Never think that," he said. "Beth and I are totally behind you all. We just want what's best." He was surprised when Edward grasped him in a hug and patted him heartily on the back. He realised Edward was trying to say thank you. He turned to Gemma as Edward released him. "How are you?" he asked.

She shrugged. "I'm glad to be home and I'm glad everyone knows what happened, but it's tough."

Matthew smiled at her reassuringly. "It will be, but at least you've got some support now."

"No one can turn the clock back, though," she said. "I can't undo what I did."

"But we can all start to look forward," he said, "as difficult as it is."

Beth appeared at the door. "Drink, anyone? Tea? Coffee?"

No one wanted a drink. Mathew felt they all wanted to resolve the future of the baby boy but weren't sure how. He could sense the tension in the air, but that didn't surprise him.

Diana spoke first. "We've talked and talked, and we've offered, begged in fact, to take the baby in and bring it up, but Gemma feels she'd have to move away permanently if we did that. We can't lose her again. I feel ashamed that you've even been asked to bring up our grandchild, but it's that or we lose Gem again. It's so difficult for us."

Edward looked at Matthew. "How do you feel about this baby business? It's a hell of a big ask."

Matthew squeezed Beth's hand. He had lost count of the hours they had spent talking it over. "We're happy to take the baby in and look after him. We both think it's too soon for Gemma to reach a permanent decision, and so we can give her the time she needs to be sure."

"I've made my decision. If you won't adopt him, I'll find another way," Gemma said. "I can't bear to look at him. I don't want him near me." She shuddered.

"We know," Matthew said. "If you still feel the same in a few months, we can go through with the adoption. At the moment, it's not an option for any of us. We're not related, and private adoptions are no longer legal. We can foster your baby and start the legal process, but adoptions take time. You need that time to heal."

He saw Diana mouth *thank you*. Edward was nodding.

"I wish you'd all accept that I know what I want."

He heard frustration and fear in her voice and was glad when Beth spoke. Gemma had always trusted Beth.

"Gemma, we know what you want now. We just can't make it happen right away, but we can foster him for you. We want to be sure you still want us to adopt him when that time comes. Once the adoption goes through, you won't be able to change your mind."

Matthew was in awe of the tenderness in Beth's voice.

"You used to love Janos, but you hate him now. You know things can change."

"I was stupid then. I've had to learn lessons fast. If Janos was his dad, I'd know he was created when I was madly in love. I could just about live with that. What I can't bear is the way he was conceived, Beth. You wouldn't watch the videos, you couldn't bring yourself to, but I did, and so did my mum. I can't unsee what they show. I don't even know which of the two fathered this baby, but I know how they fathered it and it makes me want to vomit."

Matthew's heart ached for Gemma. He had more understanding than she would ever suspect because he had helped Beth overcome similar brutality. "I'm just asking you to register the birth, leave the baby with us, and get the process started. You can come to a final decision when the time comes. In the meantime, your mum and dad can come here and spend as much time as they like with the baby and you could call in, if you ever wanted to."

"Sweetheart, that would be perfect. You must see that. Matthew and Beth are trying to make sure it's what you really want." Diana held Gemma's hand tightly.

"Gemma, you can't ask for more than this. Everyone is on your side, not just today, but for the rest of your life." Edward said. Matthew thought how worn out and sad he looked. "You've got such a long way to go to get over this. We all have."

Gemma put her head in her hands, and all Matthew was aware of was the ticking of the old clock in the hall. There was silence apart from that.

Eventually she spoke. "You're being wonderful, and I know you're talking sense. I just want this nightmare to end. I want it all to be over."

"Gemma, we have agreed to adopt him. That's a promise. We just won't be able to do it for a while," Beth said. "I love him already, and I'd adopt him tomorrow, but I'm not allowed to. And there's just a tiny chance you might change your mind. It would be tough to hand him back, but we'd do it if that's what you decided. We're trying to protect you."

"Protect me from myself?"

"Something like that," Matthew smiled. "We just don't want you looking back and regretting giving him up. None of us can see into the future."

"I do understand," she said," and I know I should be grateful, but you're all wrong. I will register his birth, but you can name him. Even that is too much for me."

Matthew could see Beth smiling. He waited for her to speak, knowing what she would say. "That is such a privilege," she said. "We'd like to call him Gethin. It's a Welsh name, like Gwyneth, and it means *little dark one.*"

He waited to see if anyone flinched at the direct reference to the baby's colour. He and Beth had chosen the name to show they embraced it and because they wanted his name to have Welsh roots, like their daughter.

"Gethin Thomas," Gemma said.

"Gethin Hooper at first," Diana said. "He needs to know he's always part of our family and what a brave woman his mother is."

Gemma's eyes filled with tears. "I'm not brave. I'm just a fool who made stupid mistakes."

"Fools don't realise they made mistakes," Beth said. "You take after your mum, and she's very wise, Gemma. Let her be Gethin's grandma without making her feel disloyal to you."

Gemma sniffed, tears running from her eyes and down her nose. "Beth, always my conscience." she said, "Gethin's lucky to have you all, even though I can't bear to look at him."

"Early days for you," Beth said. "Early days."

EPILOGUE

It was mid-winter when Alison married Brooksie in the ancient church on the Brooksley estate. The tombs of his ancestors were all there, witnessing the ceremony in stony silence from their alcoves.

It was a quiet affair. None of Brooksie's children had been invited and neither bride nor groom wanted hordes present as they made their vows. Both, for the first time, were marrying for love, and they wanted a simple and sincere occasion.

When Alison walked herself down the aisle, she had the Brooksley diamonds round her neck. They provided more brilliance to her simple cream dress than any rhinestone encrustation could have achieved. They were magnificent old cushion-cut stones in a simple platinum setting. She had told Beth she had refused to wear the Brooksley tiara, saying, in her case, there was no need to gild the lily.

Beth knew that, behind the joke was Alison's conviction she wasn't marrying Brooksie for his title.

Matthew conducted the service. It was a long time since he had put on his clerical robes. Beth was struck by how comfortable he looked in them. This was a part of his life they had never shared, and once again, she was reminded how much his calling meant to him.

She had raged against religion for a long time, feeling betrayed by what had happened to her. Now, in the sanctity of Alison's marriage ceremony, she found herself totally at peace. She had many blessings to count that had come to her since those dark days.

She had Matthew and his unfaltering support. She had Gwynnie, the child she had thought impossible. Now she had Gethin, her legally adopted son and precious second child. She lived in The Willows, the place where she felt safe and happy. She found she had a lot of thanks to give and suddenly realised there was a way she could give back.

The wedding breakfast was held in the dining room of Brooksley Hall. She sat next to Matthew, Gethin in her arms.

"You know how strongly you felt about putting The Willows to good use?" she asked as they lingered over their coffee. Matthew nodded. "I've got an idea for something we can do together."

"Go on," he said, clearly intrigued.

"A foster home," she said. "We can take in children who need emergency care or long-term fostering. I don't mind which. It would put the house to good use." Her heart skipped at the loving way he looked at her. "Josie would be in her element."

"I love you," he said. He lifted their daughter from her seat and settled her on his lap, kissing the top of her head. "Gwynnie," he said, "you have a very special mummy."

"And daddy," Beth added.

"And baby brother," Gwynnie said.

About the Author

S D Johnson always wanted to be a writer. She trained as a journalist but moved into teaching after her marriage.

After a successful career teaching Mathematics and in senior management, she moved into the country and devoted her time to writing full time.

She is an avid reader, an active member of the local writers' group, and an enthusiastic cook.

Printed in Great Britain
by Amazon

14912926R00115